New TOEIC Listening Script

*look through
①查找 ②瀏覽 ③識破：we have looked through the enemy's
tricks. 我們已經識破敵人的詭計

PART 1

①倉庫 ②手倉行
複數

1. (D) (A) The men are painting the side of a warehouse.
   (B) The men are pushing a cart down the road. 沿著路
   (C) The men are watching television and having a beer.
   (D) The men are wearing hard hats and safety vests.

工地用安全帽   反光背心

2. (B) (A) The woman is drinking tea.
   收銀機
   (B) The cashier is standing next to the cash register.
   收銀人員
   (C) The customer is looking through her purse. 錢包
   (D) The man is talking on a cell phone.

*clean up
①打掃.清理

②梳洗 ③大撈一筆：He cleaned up in the stock market last year.

3. (D) (A) The workers are cleaning up a beach. 他在年在股票市
   (B) The workers are cutting down a tree. 大撈一筆
   (C) The workers are taking down a scaffold. →①削減
   (D) The workers are repairing a road.

*repair v①修理 ②補救：He tried to repair 鷹架 ②砍倒
his mistake.

4. (D) (A) Some kids are playing a game.
   (B) Some people are at a park.
   (C) The host is offering beverages. ③恢復：It took a long
   (D) The performer is pointing at someone in the time for him to repair
   audience. 聽眾.觀眾.讀者 指著 ↗ 獲准觀見 國王 his health.
   觀見：He was granted an audience with

5. (C) (A) The boy is playing with a toy. the king.
   (B) The girl is not wearing her seatbelt.
   (C) The man is learning how to drive a truck.
   (D) The woman is riding a bicycle.

*shelf ①架子 ② The question was put on the shelf.

6. (D) (A) The saxophone is on a shelf. 被擱在一旁(不處理)
   (B) The piano is in the middle of the room.
   (C) The drums are in the alley.
   (D) The guitar is in a glass case.

GO ON TO THE NEXT PAGE.

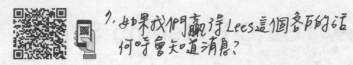

PART 2

7. 如果我們贏得Lees這個客戶的話 何呼會知道消息?

7. (C) When do you think we'll hear if we've won the Lees account?
    (A) No, we haven't found one yet. 我們還沒有找到
    (B) Because I was out of town. 我不在
    (C) Mr. Winston might already know. 他可能已經知道了

8. (A) 他沒有接受這個工作嗎? Didn't Mr. Swisher accept the job offer?
    (A) He'll let us know tomorrow. 明天跟我們說
    (B) At the board meeting next Tuesday. 在下週二的董事會議
    (C) The sales department. 銷售部門

9. (B) 我要如何知道球賽取消了呢? How will I know if the basketball game is canceled?
    (A) Have you been checked-in? 你報到了沒有?
    (B) You could look on the team's Web site. 你可以看隊伍的網頁
    (C) These seats are empty. 這些位子是空的

10. (B) 你保留了幾張桌子 How many tables did you reserve?
    (A) No, not right now.
    (B) Eight of them. 8張
    左拐近 (C) Around the corner from the office.

* The boys were swimming [around / near / about] the boat.

around   about

Victory is just around the corner. 勝利就在眼前

11. (B) Have you opened the front entrance yet? 前門入口打開了嗎?
    (A) Open a customer account. 開戶
    (B) No—I don't have a key.
    (C) It is a 10-minute walk from here. 從這裡走10分鐘

12. (C) 董事會議是幾點? board n.董事會.委員會.寄宿.牌子.木板 What time is the board meeting?
    (A) In the main conference room. 伙食: We'll provide room and board for them. 我們將會提供食宿
    (B) Her name is Susanne.
    (C) It starts at 1:30.

13. (B) ①資料夾   銷售報告 Where should I put these binders for the sales presentation?
    (A) Almost everyone signed up. 報名 ②活頁夾 (loose-leaf binder)
    (B) On the table by the door.   pastry 油酥麵團
    (C) Just coffee, tea, and some pastries.

14. (B) 我不知道要買哪個電腦型號 I don't know which computer model to buy?
    (A) Because it's running low on battery. 電力很低
    (B) What features are most important to you?
    (C) A shop in the mall. → 特色.特徵

15. (B) Who has the combination to the safe?
    (A) $500 a piece.
    (B) Your supervisor should know it.
    (C) The alarm system works well.

16. (A) Who's responsible for making hiring decisions?
    (A) The underline personnel director usually handles that.
    (B) If I have time.
    (C) Salaries are based on education and work experience.

17. (A) What's the charge to go to the hotel?
    (A) It'll cost you thirty dollars.
    (B) It needs a new handle.
    (C) You should allow half an hour.

18. (B) Which model gets the most kilometers to the liter?
    (A) About an hour's drive at the most.
    (B) The smaller one is extremely efficient.
    (C) It's a 10-kilometer race.

19. (A) When does the European Trade Conference underline take place?
    (A) During the third week of September.
    (B) Last winter in Brussels.
    (C) Since Tuesday.

20. (A) What do you think of the new reception area?
    (A) It's a definite improvement.
    (B) She seems very well qualified.
    (C) I haven't received it yet.

21. (B) When will the staff be moving to the new building?
    (A) Yes, a month ago.
    (B) In about two weeks.
    (C) For underline several hours.

22. (A) What does Miss Roberts do professionally?
    (A) She works in a law firm.
    (B) She doesn't think so.
    (C) She's talking to the professor.

GO ON TO THE NEXT PAGE.

23. (C) Which division earned the most money last quarter? 哪個部門上一季賺最多錢?
    (A) For the next year's marketing budget. 為了明年的行銷預算
    (B) By cutting the salary. 減少薪水
    (C) The Canadian sales office.

*division
n. 分開. 分割. 部門
divide
v. 分開. 劃分

你何時跟他說話的? (之前)

24. (B) When did you speak with Mr. Field?
    (A) Because it was important.
    (B) I believe it was late last week.
    (C) When he gets back to the office. (探)

*fill v. 填滿, 填滿, 滿足
→ He is the best man to fill the vacancy.
→ Her eyes filled with tears.

法務部門的職缺何時會補齊?

25. (B) When will the opening in the legal division be filled?
    (A) By advertising on the Internet. 藉由網路廣告
    (B) When Miss Junko returns from vacation. 當她度假回來
    (C) A good position for a legal assistant. 法務助理的好職位

*be filled with 充滿
反 be empty of

勞工糾紛何時會達到解決(有結果)?

26. (B) When did the labor dispute reach a resolution?
    (A) We should get there by lunchtime.
    (B) The issue was settled late last night.
    (C) Yes, everyone seemed to agree on the terms.

*dispute
第2篇. 爭執

*labor
n. ①勞工. 勞動 ②工作表現: He likes your labor.
③分娩: The woman is in labor.
v. ①勞動: She labored 10 years on that book.
②費力前進: The train labored up the hill.
adj. 勞工的. 工會的

誰將會取代派克先生?

27. (A) Who's going to replace Mr. Park?
    (A) Someone from the regional office.
    (B) Please return it to the clerk.
    (C) He doesn't want to travel so much.

→ replace 取代. 償還 I'll replace the cup I broke.

誰要搬去三樓的辦公室?

28. (A) Who is going to move into the offices on the third floor?
    (A) A small law firm has just signed a lease. 一個小的法律公司剛簽了租約
    (B) Not more than five. 不超過5個
    (C) Almost 50 euros per square foot. 每呎差不多50歐

*condition
n. 情況 ①環境 ②條件: I'll do it on condition that you pay for everything.
v. 決定. 為~的條件
Ability and effort condition success.
能力和努力是決定成功的條件

行李提領處在哪裡?

29. (B) Where is the baggage claim area?
    (A) Not without your receipt. 沒有你的收據就不行
    (B) Go straight down to the first floor. 直接下一樓
    (C) No, I have two large suitcases.

哪裡可以找到這台冷氣機的替換濾心

30. (C) Where can I get a replacement filter for this air-conditioner?
    (A) By the end of the month.
    (B) Yes, fill it up to the top. fill up 填滿, 裝滿
    (C) Order one from the catalogue.

調節器
濾發素

31. (A) Why aren't any of the computer terminals turned on? 為什麼沒有任電腦終端開啟?

　　(A) The new hardware system is being installed this morning. 新的硬體系統

　　(B) Yes, I turned them on when I arrived today. 今天早上被安裝了。

　　(C) Because this bus terminal is always so busy. 因為這個

adj. 終點的 terminal station/stop
晚期的 terminal cancer
n. 總站. 航度. 終點. 極限

PART 3

Questions 32 through 34 refer to the following conversation.

M : Hello, I'm calling about a door I'm repairing for you. I wanted to order the exact same door knob to replace the one that's missing, but it is no longer available. So you have to choose a different one. 訂購　確切的　一樣的門把　在你前窗的展示(陳列)中　不再　可取得了

W : That's OK. I remember seeing a door knob in your shop that I like. It's round and silver and found on display in your front window. Do you think you could use that instead? 圓的　銀的　你覺得可以用那個代替嗎?

M : Sure, but I will have to order one because I don't have another one in stock. So the repair won't be done for another two weeks. 我沒有另外的庫存　所以維修工作二週之內不會完成

32. (D) Why is the man calling the woman?

　　(A) To discuss a consultation. 討論一個商討(諮詢)
　　(B) To provide a business address. 提供營業地址
　　(C) To promote new service. 推出新服務
　　(D) To discuss a repair. 討論一個維修

* promote 促進, 推銷, 發起

33. (D) What does the woman describe? 女生形容什麼?

　　(A) Some window designs. 一些窗戶設計
　　(B) A room arrangement. 一個房間的安排
　　(C) A paint color. 油漆顏色
　　(D) A door knob. 門把

* profit
n. 利潤. 利益. 收益
v. 有益於
→ Telling lies won't profit you.
說謊對你沒好處
得益

34. (A) What does the man say he has to do?

　　(A) Order some items. 訂購一些商品
　　(B) Extend a warranty. 延長保固
　　(C) Offer a discount. 提供折扣
　　(D) Mail some samples. 寄送試用品

→ He learned to profit by his mistakes.
學會從自己的錯誤中獲益(學習)

Questions 35 through 37 refer to the following conversation.

總體上　銷售數字　遠少於　旅遊指南　烹飪書

M : Dina, have you seen our sales figures? We sold a lot fewer travel guides and cookbooks last quarter. And overall, our profits are down 17 percent. 利潤下降17%

GO ON TO THE NEXT PAGE.

49

W : Foot traffic has been down in all our locations. I don't know if that's a reflection of the economy or what. 訪人常來的交通（不開車火城的人數）人數變少了。不知道是經濟的反應還是什麼

M : I've been saying this for a long time, but we need to start selling books from our Web site.

W : Well, Tim, we agreed at the beginning of this venture that we would not get into online commerce, and I think we need to stick with our brick-and-mortar business model.

說話者最有可能是誰
35. (D) Who most likely are the speakers?　ㄓ磚　ㄣ灰漿
　　　(A) Authors. 作者
　　　(B) Magazine editors. 雜誌編輯　實際存在的.有敞有房的公司
　　　(C) Software developers. 軟體研發　冒險.投機活動
　　　(D) Bookstore owners.
　　　　　書店老闆

36. (C) What does the man suggest doing? 這個男生建議做什麼？
launch　(A) Drafting an article for a magazine. 為一個雜誌文章起草
使船下水　(B) Rescheduling a product launch. 一個商品推出日期重新安排行程
發射.發動　(C) Selling products on the Internet. 網路上賣商品
發起　(D) Reviewing a publishing contract. 審查一個出版的合約

37. (C) What does the woman object to? 這個女生反對什麼？ object v.反對
　　　(A) Ordering additional merchandise. 訂購多的商品　'object n.目標
　　　(B) Opening another store.
　　　(C) Changing the business model. 改變商業模式
　　　(D) Spending on advertisement. 花錢在廣告上

Questions 38 through 40 refer to the following conversation.
齒模　　　　　　　　　　　牙齒的.牙科的　examination 檢查.考試
W : Hi, this is Yolanda Peters calling. I was in your office for a dental exam last week and ordered a new mouth guard. I was told to call back today to check whether it is ready.

M : Hello, Ms. Peters. We will have it ready for you later today. You can come in any time after two o'clock to pick it up. 我被告知今天打電話回來問看齒模好了沒有
順道經過
W : Okay, great. I can stop by before you close. Could you tell me how the discount coupon works? I received one when I had my teeth cleaned here last time. Can I use it for this purchase? 我上次來清洗牙齒的時候收到這張優惠券

M : Yes, since the cost of this order is over one hundred dollars. You can use it to get 50% off the total price. Just present the coupon when you pay. 超過
展示

38. (D) Why is the woman calling?　　　　　＊ inquire　about 詢問
　　　(A) To get driving directions. 問方向　　　　into 調查
　　　(B) To inquire about a job.　　　　　　　　for 求見
　　　(C) To make an appointment. 預約
　　　(D) To check on an order. 查看一筆訂單

50

39. (D) What does the woman say she will do?
 (A) Call her insurance company. 打給她的保險公司
 (B) Consult another doctor. 咨詢另外一位醫生
 (C) Send an application. 寄送申請表
 (D) Visit an office.

40. (A) What does the man explain? (得到)
 (A) How to receive a discount. 如何收到一個折扣
 (B) How to obtain medical records.
 (C) How to repair an item. 如何修理一個品項
 (D) How to check an account status. 如何檢查一個帳號(戶)狀態

Questions 41 through 43 *refer to the following conversation.*

繳交　　　申請表

W : Hi, I'd like to submit this application for a Chinese business visa. I'm hoping to leave for Shanghai next week.
expedite v. 促進,加快　　v. 處理,加工
M : Well, I suggest you pay for the expedited service. We will process your application today. And you can back to pick up your business visa tomorrow.
2a n. 簽證 v. 在護照上用簽證
W : That's great. I will be able to take my trip then. Do I pay you for that faster service?
M : No, you need to go to window 10 to pay the processing fee. Only cash or credit cards are accepted. In the process 在進行中　　處理費

41. (B) What is the woman trying to do?
 (A) Book a hotel. 預訂一間旅館
apply to (B) Apply for a visa. 申請簽証
適用於 (C) Open an account. 開戶 ——→ n. 帳戶,帳戶,描述,解釋,說明
 (D) Send a package. 寄送包裏
→ He gave us a detailed account of his plan.

n. I obtained a visa to visit Thailand.
v. I had my passport visaed.

42. (C) What does the man recommend? 建議(推薦)
 (A) Reading some instructions. 閱讀一些指導方針
 (B) Requesting a receipt. 要求收據
 (C) Using a faster service. 使用快速服務
 (D) Choosing a different date. 選擇不一樣的日期

v. 把…視為
解釋,說明 + for
→ He was accounted a first-rate actor.
他被視為一流演員

43. (D) What can the woman do at window 10?
 (A) Speak to a supervisor. 和長官(主管)說
 (B) Receive a voucher. 收到一張禮券
 (C) Have her photograph taken. 拍照
 (D) Pay a fee. 付錢

→ He could not account for his absence from school.
他沒辦法解釋他沒去學校的事.

GO ON TO THE NEXT PAGE.

W : Grant? It's Rebecca. I've just missed my flight back to Nashville. I'll have to spend another night in L.A., and I'm booked on another 3:00 p.m. flight, so I won't make it into the office tomorrow. 明天無法到辦公室

M : Hmm, I was counting on you being here tomorrow at 9:00 a.m. for an important meeting. Do you think you could arrange to meet through a video-conferencing? 視訊會議

W : Well, there is a business center here in the hotel. But I'm not sure if it's equipped for video-conferencing. Let me go down there and see if the center has the necessary equipment.

44. (D) What problem does the woman inform the man about?
   (A) She lost her computer.
   (B) Her luggage did not arrive. 行李沒到
   (C) Her password is incorrect. 密碼不對
   (D) She missed a flight. 錯過班機

45. (C) What does the man suggest?
   (A) Consulting a travel agency. 咨詢旅行社
   (B) Using a car service to visit a client.
   (C) Joining a meeting by video-conference.
   (D) Returning to a hotel.

46. (A) What does the woman plan to do next?
   (A) Check for some equipment. 檢查設備
   (B) Call an airline. 打給航空公司
   (C) Report a complaint. 繳交抱怨表(申訴表)
   (D) Go to a repair shop. 修理東西的店

equip 配備. 使有能力
Our lab is well equipped.
→ Your training will equip you for your future job.
→ equipment 設備. 才能, 知識. 素養
We never doubted his equipment for this important position.
equipage n. 船. 軍隊. 探險隊的 裝備.用具

complaint
①抱怨 ②不舒服
Arthritis is a common /aɪˈθraɪtɪs/ complaint 關節炎 among the elderly.

Woman UK : Hey, guys. I need a minute with you because I'm writing up the new employee training manual we'll be discussing at tomorrow's meeting.

Man Canada : Oh, hi, Laura. I got an e-mail this morning saying that the meeting has been rescheduled for next week. 重新安排到下周3喊

Man Aus : Yeah, me too. 對我來說是新聞(我不知道)

Woman UK : That's news to me. I'll get a hold of Brad Palmer and see what that's about, but the training manual remains a pressing concern. So, I'd like to get some feedback and suggestions from both of you. 緊急要處理的事

→ 以電話跟某人取得聯繫 朝聖者

n. 手冊, 簡介 adj. 體力的 我需要佔用你一點時間

→ manual labor

Man Canada : Well, I'm really jammed for time this morning, since I have a deadline on the contract for the recycling project.

Woman UK : How about you, George?

Man Aus : I'm dealing with a backlog of orders in the warehouse. But if you give me the draft, I will be happy to take a look at it right after lunch.

47. (B) What is the woman preparing?
    (A) Some order forms.
    (B) Some training materials.
    (C) A meeting agenda.
    (D) An office newsletter.

48. (C) Why did the woman say, "That's news to me"?
    (A) She had already booked a conference room.
    (B) She thought a delivery had been made.
    (C) She was unaware that a meeting had been postponed.
    (D) She believed that policy had changed.

49. (B) What does George agree to do after lunch?
    (A) Sign an agreement.
    (B) Review a document.
    (C) Confirm a deadline.
    (D) Email a colleague.

Questions 50 through 52 refer to the following conversation between three speakers.

Man : Our clothes are selling really well, so the company has decided to expand our market into Latin America and sell our product line there, too. They're hiring a new regional manager. Do either of you have any interest in the job?

Woman UK : I might, but do you know any details about the job?

Man : Well, the job posting says retail stores will be opening in Panama, Brazil, and possibly other countries later on. They are looking for someone to oversee the operation of the new stores. Don't you speak Spanish, Paula?

Woman US : Yes, I speak decent Spanish and have spent time in Latin America, so I would probably be an asset in working with the staff there. I may be qualified.

Man : That's great! How about you, Wendy? Any interest in the job?

Woman UK : I don't speak a foreign language and I've never traveled abroad, so it might not be a good fit for me.

GO ON TO THE NEXT PAGE.

53

50. (D) What type of company do the speakers work for?

    (A) A travel agency. 旅行社

    (B) A furniture manufacturer. 家俱製造商

    (C) An interior design firm. 室內設計公司 interior ↔ exterior

    (D) A clothing retailer. 衣服零售商

根據這個人   這個職位的主要責任

51. (C) According to the man, what is the main responsibility of the position?

    (A) Supervising an assembly line. 組裝線 supervise v. 監督、管理

    (B) Developing a sales strategy. 發展銷售策略 上面 see 略

    (C) Managing multiple stores. 管理多家的店

    (D) Creating product designs. 創作產品設計

能力/資格   *expert /ˈɛkspɚt/

52. (B) What qualification does Paula mention?

    (A) She has a large number of clients.

     n.專家、能手 adj. 訓練的、有經驗的

    (B) She speaks a foreign language.

    (C) She is familiar with the company's products. =adept =skillful

    (D) She is an expert in retail trends 零售趨勢 =professional =handy

     =master =proficient

     =masterful

***Questions 53 through 55** refer to the following conversation.*

超想知道

M : So, how was the meeting with the designers? I'm dying to know what you think of the new autumn clothing line. n.秋天、季 adj.秋天的 *made from 本質有改變

W : Well, I'm wearing a pair of the leggings. They're made of 95 percent cotton and 5 percent polyester, and they're really quite comfortable. 本質上沒有改變 =The chair is made of wood.

     ɑ 聚酯纖維

M : That's a great selling point! Let's make comfort the central focus of our advertising campaign. 很棒的賣點   我們讓(把)舒適度成為主要的重點

     廣告宣傳的

53. (D) What industry do the speakers most likely work in?

    (A) Advertising.

    (B) Energy. 能源   *legging 緊身彈力褲

    (C) Tourism. 旅遊   pantyhose 褲襪

    (D) Fashion. 流行   stockings 長筒襪

54. (A) What does the woman say about a new product? socks 一般襪子

    (A) It is comfortable.

    (B) It is inexpensive. 不貴

    (C) It is selling well. 賣很好

    (D) It is being redesigned. 重新設計過

55. (B) What does the man suggest?
    (A) Arranging a press conference.
    (B) Promoting a special feature.
    (C) Initiating product testing.
    (D) Giving away free samples.

*initiate v. 開始 adj. 新加入的 n. 新加入者

Questions 56 through 58 *refer to the following conversation.*

W : I'm excited about Lathrop's plan to bring in more customers. I've seen the upcoming ad campaign, and I think it will be really effective in attracting new business.

M : Yes, I agree, as long as we schedule to run print ads in June issues of selected magazines.

W : Right, and we launch the television ad campaign after that in July. But I hear there are still some discussions about whether to focus the television ads on Internet banking or home loans.

M : I think that Internet banking would appeal more to the type of customers we are looking for. And on television, they are really able to visualize all the features of the system.

I can't visualize his face.

56. (C) What are the speakers mainly discussing?
    (A) The announcement of a new manager.
    (B) The introduction of a special service.
    (C) Plans for increasing business.
    (D) Procedures for a departmental process.

57. (A) What will happen in July?
    launch 船下水、發射、開始
    (A) Television advertisements will be launched.
    (B) Client testimonials will be posted online.
    (C) A new Internet bank will be established.
    (D) An advertising agency will be hired.

58. (D) What does the man say will appeal to customers?
    (A) Foreign currency exchange. ① 訴諸: You should not appeal to force.
    (B) Extended business hours. 不應訴諸武力
    (C) Home loans. ② 有吸引力、迎合口味
    (D) Online banking.

Questions 59 through 61 *refer to the following conversation.*

M : Welcome back to the Business Network, I'm your host, Jack Lee. In our studio today, Sophia Rizzo, president and CEO of Quasar Motors, (Kwesar) is here to discuss her company's new eco-friendly car. Sophia, what can you tell us about your new product?

GO ON TO THE NEXT PAGE.

W : Our new car, the Oasia, will be the first vehicle to run solely on compressed air. This technology has been around for many years, but this is the first car that doesn't also use gasoline or electricity for fuel.

M : You're kidding! That's amazing. So how far along are you in the production process? When will the car be available?

W : The final testing of the pre-production models will be completed in a few months. So expect that 6 months from now, the first Oasia will be on the market.

59. (B) Who is Sophia Rizzo?
   (A) A television producer.
   (B) A car company president.
   (C) An aircraft designer.
   (D) An electrical engineer.

60. (D) Why does the man say, "You're kidding!"?
   (A) He strongly disagrees.
   (B) He would like an explanation.
   (C) He feels disappointed.
   (D) He is happily surprised.

61. (A) According to the woman, what will happen in six months?
   (A) A vehicle will be available for purchase.
   (B) A new television series will begin.
   (C) A business update will be published.
   (D) Production costs will increase.

Questions 62 through 64 *refer to the following conversation and list of passengers.*

W : Hi, I'm one of the names listed on your sign. Tara Crover, with Goldstar Incorporated. I'm here for the electronics convention. I take it you're going to drive us to the hotel. Have any of my colleagues arrived yet?

M : Welcome to San Francisco, Ms. Crover. You're the first to arrive. I believe your associate from Chicago is due to arrive shortly. Unfortunately, your colleagues coming from Atlanta have been delayed. Their flight was re-routed through Pittsburgh.

W : When are they expected to arrive?

M : Not until 8:30 this evening.

W : Um, we'll miss the opening reception if we wait for them.

M : We won't. We'll only wait for your colleague coming from Chicago. I'll drive the two of you to the hotel and then return for the others. Here——let me take your bag to the waiting area.

62. (C) What is the purpose of the woman's trip? 這位女士旅行的目的是什麼?
   (A) To negotiate a contract. negotiate
   (B) To visit family. 談判、協商、洽談
   (C) To attend a trade show. 貿易展 Both sides still refuse to come to the negotiating table.
   (D) To interview for a job.
   (雙方仍拒絕談判)
   討論工資、條件的會議

63. (D) Look at the graphic. Who will arrive next?
   (A) Alan Wurtz.
   (B) Hope Dane-Wallace.
   (C) Tara Crover.
   (D) Francisco De La Rosa.

incorporated

SAROVAR HOTELS & RESORTS **GOLDSTAR INC.**

Name	Departure City
Mr. Alan Wurtz	Atlanta
Ms. Hope Dane-Wallace	Atlanta
Ms. Tara Crover	Denver
Mr. Francisco De La Rosa	Chicago

男生說可以幫女生做什麼?
64. (C) What does the man offer to do for the woman?
   (A) Pay a fee. 付錢
   (B) Buy some coffee.   *indicate
   (C) Carry her luggage. 提行李   v. 指出、表明、暗示
   (D) Give her a massage. 按摩   → His hesitation indicates unwillingness.
                                       他的猶豫表明不願意

Questions 65 through 67 refer to the following conversation and bulletin board posting.
                                社區   公告欄
W : Hi, I'm calling about a post on the community bulletin board indicating you're selling a
   camping tent. Could you tell me more about it? 6 x 15 英呎 = 30.48 cm 顏色是水藍色
M : Sure, it's a Moleman 6-Person Weather Chief. Six by 15 feet. Aqua blue in color. I'm only
   asking a hundred for it. Do you want to come and have a look at it?

W : I would but I'm on my way out of town for a few days. Can you e-mail some pictures? If I
   like it, I can stop by and pick it up on the way home from my trip.
     順道拜訪
M : I can do that. I'll send it to you shortly. What's your e-mail address?
        立刻、馬上、不久

GO ON TO THE NEXT PAGE.

65. (A) Why is the woman calling?

(A) To inquire about an item.

(B) To cancel a purchase.

(C) To report a lost item.

(D) To get driving directions.

66. (C) Look at the graphic? Who is the woman speaking with?

(A) John Moss.

(B) Vicki Wang.

(C) Fred Gustavson.

(D) Beth Grant.

BROOKFIELD COMMUNITY BULLETIN BOARD
WANTED: Used clothing, books, appliances – please call John Moss at St. Mark's Mission (202) 434-9090
Piano Lessons – Group or private – Best rates – Vicki Wang (202) 213-3444
For Sale: Kommander Weather Chief 6-Person Camping Tent. 6' x 15' – $100 – Good condition. Call Fred Gustavson (202) 213-0771
Volunteer Abroad! Many fulfilling opportunities with Frontier Foundation. (202) 434-2332. Call now! Ask for Beth Grant

67. (D) What does the man say he will e-mail?

(A) An itinerary.

(B) A contract.

(C) Some instructions.

(D) Some images.

Questions 68 through 70 refer to the following conversation and guide.

M : Hello, this is my first visit to your café. Can you recommend a coffee drink for me?

W : Sure, what kind of coffee do you usually enjoy? Latte? Cappuccino? Americano?

M : I've only ever had regular brewed coffee. But my co-worker told me that you make some really tasty drinks. So I think I'd like to try something new. Do you make anything with chocolate?

58

W : We sure do! We have several options, but I'd recommend the café mocha. We're actually having a promotion on our specialty drinks. If you buy one, you'll get half off your next purchase.

我們當然有

adj.特色的 r place n.專業、專長、特色、特產 store

M : Great, I'd like to try one. Does it cost the same as the other drinks?

W : It's not our most expensive item. Here's a price list for you. *purchase

68. (A) Why does the man want to try a new drink?
   (A) It was recommended by a co-worker.
   (B) It was featured in a news report. 在新聞報導中有出現
   (C) He's on a diet. 在減肥
   (D) It has health benefits. 有健康方面的好處

   *feature
   n.特徵、特色
   v.以…為名

69. (C) What will the man receive with his purchase?
   (A) A pastry.
   (B) A membership card.
   (C) A discount on his next purchase.
   (D) A gift certificate.

   certificate
   n.證書、執照   v.給證明書、認可
   = testimonial
   = certification
   禮券

70. (C) Look at the graphic. How much did the man pay for his drink?
   (A) 2.50.
   (B) 3.00.
   (C) 3.50.
   (D) 4.00.

   *purchase
   v.買回努力得來
   → We treasure this dearly purchased victory.
   我們珍惜這得來不易的勝利
   n.買、所購之物
   緊抓 = He got a purchase on a branch(樹枝) until we come to his rescue.
   他緊抓樹枝直到我們去救他

Beverage	Price
Latte	2.50
Cappuccino	3.00
Café Mocha	3.50
Café Miel	4.00

GO ON TO THE NEXT PAGE.

*various adj. 不同的. 各種各樣的. 形形色色的
→ He has various reasons for being late. 花式遲到理由

Questions 71 through 73 refer to the following announcement.

→ Apple is grown in various parts of the country.

Welcome aboard this afternoon's Jet King flight 5J311 non-stop to Little Rock. While we taxi to the runway, I'd like to tell you about a new service offered by Jet King Airlines. In addition to movies and music, you can now access digital versions of a wide variety of magazines from the entertainment module on the seat-back in front of you. You'll be able to read current and previous issues of a range of magazines using the touchscreen monitor. If you'd like to use this service, just swipe your credit card to get started.

71. (A) Where is the announcement being made?
(A) On an airplane.
(B) On a tour bus.
(C) At a bank.
(D) At a theater.

*deal n. 交易. 大量 He has a great deal of thought.
v. 發牌. 交易, 處理 +with
It's his turn to deal.
The store deals in silk. 這家店賣絲

72. (B) What service is the speaker mainly explaining?
(A) Personal concierge. 門房
(B) Digital entertainment.
(C) Food options.
(D) Discount tickets.

*afford ↗ I can't afford to buy the bag.
① 買得起, 付得起的 ～+to V
② 提供: Dancing affords us pleasure.
③ 不能冒險 I can't afford to pay such a high price.

73. (D) What does the speaker say the listeners should do to use a service?
(A) Open an account.
(B) Sign up in advance. 較: ahead of time (schedule)
(C) Download a mobile app.
(D) Enter credit card information.

Questions 74 through 76 refer to the following broadcast.

You're listening to 'Access Houston'——the podcast for entrepreneurs and small business owners in Houston. One thing all business owners big or small need is good accounting software to keep track of their inventory. Today I'll be reviewing a few accounting software programs that I've worked with over the years, but right now I want to remind you that this podcast is made possible by the generous support of our sponsor, Wizard Solutions. If you're in the market for affordable and reliable Web hosting, visit the Wizard Solutions Web site for the latest promotional deals.

74. (A) Who is the intended audience of the podcast?
(A) Small business owners.
(B) Corporate trainers.
(C) Civil engineers.
(D) Health-care professionals.

75. (C) What will the speaker discuss on today's show?
(A) Leadership skills.
(B) Real Estate.
(C) Accounting software.
(D) Customer relations.

76. (B) What does the speaker suggest the listeners do?
(A) Enter a contest.
(B) Visit a Web site.
(C) Submit their questions.
(D) Attend an event.

Questions 77 through 79 *refer to the following instructions.*

Good morning! My name is Rick and I'm the maintenance foreman at our factory. Our new sheet metal cutting equipment was installed by technicians last night. These machines can cut up to 10 layers of sheet metal at once, which will make all of your jobs a little easier and expedite the process on the factory production line. For optimal results, the gears of each machine will need to be cleaned every day——ideally, at the beginning of each shift. I've posted a maintenance schedule at each cutting station. Now, if someone will use the dolly to roll that bolt of steel over here, I'll demonstrate how these machines work.

77. (C) Where does the talk most likely take place?
(A) At a trade show.
(B) At a dry-cleaning store.
(C) At a factory.
(D) At a repair shop.

78. (D) What are the listeners advised to do every day?
(A) Use industrial earplugs.
(B) Take inventory.
(C) Meet production quotas.
(D) Clean some equipment.

GO ON TO THE NEXT PAGE

79. (A) What does the speaker say he will do next?
- (A) Give a demonstration. 做一個展示
- (B) Distribute a questionnaire. 分發一張問卷調查表
- (C) Introduce a visitor. 介紹一個拜訪者
- (D) Take a short break. 休息一下

distribute
v. 分發、分配
questionnaire
/ˈkwɛstʃənɛr/
①開的、調查表

Questions 80 through 82 refer to the following talk.

我感謝大家準時參加員工會議　kick off ①開球　開始之前

Hey guys. I appreciate everybody being on time for the staff meeting. To kick things off, I have the honor of awarding the Salesperson of the Month to Harrison Camp. Harrison's been leading our business-to-business division for three years now, and most recently worked on our social media campaign. Harrison was responsible for increasing our company's visibility by posting ads on popular sites. Thanks to his work, in the past month we've generated 15% more sales leads from people signing up for our email newsletter. On top of that, next week Harrison will be leading an in-house seminar on marketing innovation. Please give a warm welcome to Harrison Camp, our Salesperson of the Month.

本月最佳銷售員　B to B　部門
社群媒體宣傳活動　員
增加　①能見度　藉由張貼廣告在受歡迎的網站上　由於他的努力
引起、達成、廣告
訴說我們的電子報
內部的研討會
除此之外
行銷改革
innovate v. 創立、革新

80. (D) What is the purpose of the talk? 這則說話的目的是?
- (A) To welcome a new employee. 歡迎新員工
- (B) To celebrate a corporate merger. 合併
- (C) To remind staff of a policy.
- (D) To announce an award winner. 宣佈一個得獎者

innovation n. 改革、創新、新方法
remind sb. of sth. 使想起(提醒)

81. (B) What does the speaker say has recently increased?
- (A) Local taxes. 當地稅　→ email. phone, 會議、展覽、活動、廣告等²
- (B) Sales leads. 銷售的線索→機會→業績
- (C) Quarterly travel spending. 季度的旅行開支
- (D) Insurance deductibles. 可減免(扣除)的東西　deduct v. 扣除、減除

82. (A) What will Harrison Camp be doing next week?
- (A) Leading a seminar.
- (B) Launching a product.
- (C) Attending a convention.
- (D) Hiring an assistant. 雇用助手

* visibility n. 能見度
visible adj. 可見的、顯而易見的
vision n. 幻想、視力、洞察力
visage /ˈvɪzɪdʒ/ n. 容貌

Hi Chelsea, it's Amelia. I'm calling about the new food processor model. As you know, we've scheduled the first round of consumer focus groups. While we're always concerned about having people review a model that's still in the development stage, keep in mind that we'll only be asking participants about the appearance of the food processor at this point. You can continue to work out the remaining details in terms of the interior electronics. Then, once your department is ready with a prototype, we'll definitely hold a second round of focus groups. Meanwhile, could you please let me know the date you think your team will be ready for the first round?

83. (B) Where does the speaker most likely work?
   (A) At a culinary academy.
   (B) At an electronics manufacturer.
   (C) At an advertising firm.
   (D) At an appliance store.

84. (A) Why does the speaker say, "We'll only be asking reviewers about the appearance of the food processor at this point"?
   (A) To reassure the listener about a mutual concern.
   (B) To show disappointment in a decision.
   (C) To suggest a change in product design.
   (D) To clarify that a deadline has passed.

85. (D) What does the speaker ask the listener to do?
   (A) Give a presentation.
   (B) Design a prototype.
   (C) Create an advertisement.
   (D) Provide a date.

Attention shoppers. Head on over to the Bake Shop where you can sample our new line of delicious gluten-free bakery items. I understand Landon has just baked a fresh batch of oatmeal cookies. Our gluten-free recipes are more flavorful than other bakeries because there's nothing artificial added to the organic flour substitute we use. And this week only we're selling all gluten-free items at a 20 percent discount.

GO ON TO THE NEXT PAGE.

86. (C) Where is the announcement being made?
    (A) In an airport.
    (B) At a job fair. 工作展
    (C) At a supermarket.
    (D) In a restaurant.

roast
v. 烘：The sun was roasting us.
太陽晒太 (好熱)
→ teach one's grandmother to roast eggs 班門弄斧

演講者鼓勵聽眾做什麼?

87. (D) What does the speaker invite the listeners to do?
    (A) Pick up a coupon. 拿起/撿起一張折價券
    (B) Get in a line. 排隊
    (C) Purchase a membership. 買會員 (入會)
    (D) Try a sample. 試吃 (用)

→ They got roasted for losing the game 痛宰

88. (C) According to the speaker, why do the bakery items taste better?
    (A) They are made with special equipment. 用特殊設備做的
    (B) The beans are roasted locally. 豆子是當地烘烤的
    (C) They have no chemical additives. 沒有化學的添加劑
    (D) They were imported from another country. 從別的國家進口

import ↔ export

Questions 89 through 91 refer to an excerpt from a meeting. 嚴厲的

由於我們對于在市場的存在感 (曝光) 已經很強

It shouldn't surprise any of us that our company's been facing stiff competition in recent
面臨到 硬的·挺的·困難的
months. Since our competitors have been establishing a strong presence in the market,
establish 建立 n. 存在
in order to gain a competitive edge, it's essential that everyone in this department hone
為了 達到 競爭 優勢 必要的·不可缺的
their marketing skills. So I scheduled a professional development workshop next
化坊研討會
Thursday at 2 o'clock. Some of you may have other meetings scheduled at that time, 磨練·鍛
對我們公司未來發展很重要 研討會之後 練
but this is important to our company's future. Following the seminar, I'll send you a form
詳細的回饋
asking for your detailed feedback. Please be sure to complete it and send it to me within
24 hours after you receive it. 24小時之內

根據說話者,最近幾個月發生什麼事?

89. (A) According to the speaker, what has happened in recent months?
    (A) Competition from other companies has increased. 增加
    (B) Employees have reported low job satisfaction. 工作滿意度很低
    (C) Manufacturing goals have not been met. 製造目標沒有達到
    (D) A product release has been delayed. 產品延期推出
    ┼ loosen

90. (B) What should listeners send to the speaker? v. 解開·釋放·解脫·發表
    (A) A list of client contacts. 聯絡名單 放棄
    (B) A feedback form.
    (C) A travel itinerary. 旅遊行程表 → He released his claim to the property.
    (D) Expense reports. 花費報告 放棄了對財產的要求
    → A new movie is to be released tonight.
    發行·發表

64

91. (D) What does the speaker imply when she says, "This is important to our company's future"?

adj. 替代的 n. 可供選擇的東西(辦法) What alternatives are there?

    (A) She hopes to find an alternative solution. 有其他的選擇嗎?

    (B) She wants to recognize the listeners' efforts 努力

    (C) She wants to accommodate a client's request. 滿足(符合)客戶的需求

    (D) She expects employees to attend a seminar.

預期(希望)員工參加研討會　認出,認可,承諾: I recognized that I had made a mistake.

Questions 92 through 94 refer to the following tour information.

斷定,結束　　　　　天文台,瞭望所

And this concludes our tour of the White Beach Observatory. I hope it's been both educational and entertaining. Before you leave today, why not stop by our gift shop? We have a large selection of T-shirts, postcards, and calendars. As a public institution, 公家單位 we're partially funded by the purchases you make. Also, you may be interested in learning more about our Young Astronomer programs. Our education specialist, Olivia, is at the front desk.

天文學家　astrology n. 占星術
star
'astronaut n. 太空人　　　'institute stand
astronomy n. 天文學　　v. 創立,設立,著手
aeronautics n. 航空學　　n. 學會,校,慣例

92. (A) Who most likely is the speaker?

    (A) A tour guide.

    (B) A sales clerk.

    (C) A scientist.

    (D) A corporate executive.

93. (D) What does the speaker suggest that the listeners do before leaving?

    (A) Apply for a membership. 申請會員　＊ -ist ～主義者,從事～的專家

    (B) Fill out a survey. 填寫問查表　feminist n. 女權議者 (feminine 女性的)

    (C) Watch a short film. 看短影片　florist n. 花商.

    (D) Go to a gift shop. 去禮品店　'humanist n. 人道義者

94. (B) Why does the speaker say, "Our education specialist, Olivia, is at the front desk"?

    (A) To request volunteers. 要求自願者　indicate　idealist n. 理想主義者

    (B) To indicate where to get information. v 指示,指出　'sophist n. 詭辯家

    (C) To deny a visitor's request. 拒絕拜訪者的要求　學者

    (D) To explain why she must leave.　'oculist n. 眼科醫師

Questions 95 through 97 refer to the following advertisement and price list.

舉辦　年度拍賣

It's February and that means Baker's Furniture is hosting its annual sale, and right now our very popular dining room table is on sale for 75% off the original price!

打25折

GO ON TO THE NEXT PAGE.

This deal is valid for in-store purchases only. You can just pick it up from the store. All of the parts are included in one small box. Our customers love this dining room table because it can be assembled at home quickly and easily. Just log on to our Web site to access our simple assembly instructions. Don't miss out on this deal! Come visit us at Baker's Furniture today.

95. (D) Look at the graphic. What is the sale price of the table being described?
  (A) $180.
  (B) $250.
  (C) $275.
  (D) $300.

Item	Original Price	Sale Price
Dining room table	$1,200	$300
Coffee table	$540	$180
Patio table	$1,000	$250
Kitchen table	$1,100	$275

96. (C) According to the speaker, why do customers like the table?
  (A) It is hand-made.
  (B) It is available in many colors.
  (C) It is easy to assemble.
  (D) It is inexpensive.

97. (A) What does the speaker say can be found on a Web site?
  (A) Some instructions.
  (B) Some recipes.
  (C) A warranty.
  (D) A coupon.

Questions 98 through 100 refer to the following telephone message and weather report.

Hey Lindsey, this is Dylan. I'm calling about the music festival we've been planning to help raise funds for breast cancer awareness. Got a problem here, Lindsey. Have you seen the weather forecast? Apparently, it's supposed to be unseasonably hot on the day we were planning to hold our event. Over 112 degrees. Even with the use of industrial fans on stage, none of the performers will want to play under those

66

conditions. So, I'd like you to get the team together tomorrow sometime to get things in order for an alternate date. Could you organize that? It's mostly minor planning adjustments that we'll need to make.

另外的日期　可以安排嗎?　把事情用好
alternate　*如工*　*計劃*
調整　*交替的·輪流的;間隔的*　*較小的*

98. (D) What event is being discussed?

→ They see each other on alternate Sundays.
他們每隔一個星期天相會一次

 (A) A grand opening.

 (B) A charity walk.

 (C) A trip to the zoo.

 (D) A music festival.

adj·生動的·圖解的

99. (C) Look at the graphic. Which day was the event originally scheduled for?

 (A) Thursday.　*又 工*

 (B) Friday.　*＊scattered*　*＊onshore*

 (C) Saturday.　*adj·散亂的·散布的*　*adj·向陸地的*　*吹向*

 (D) Sunday.　*多雲+潮溼　小雨+零星雷雨　超熱　暖和的+陸上的風*
(通常夏天吹此風)

Weather Forecast			
Thursday	Friday	Saturday	Sunday
Cloudy and humid	Light rain with scattered thunderstorms	Extreme heat	Sunny with onshore winds
High: 85	High: 90	High: 112+	High: 92
Low: 75	Low: 80	Low: 88	Low: 81

100. (A) What does the speaker ask the listener to do?

 (A) Arrange a meeting.　*安排一個會議*

 (B) Contact scheduled performers.　*聯絡安排好的表演者*

 (C) Rent industrial fans.　*租用工業用扇*

 (D) Print new tickets.　*印新的票券*

GO ON TO THE NEXT PAGE.

READING TEST

In the Reading test, you will read a variety of texts and answer several different types of reading comprehension questions. The entire Reading test will last 75 minutes. There are three parts, and directions are given for each part. You are encouraged to answer as many questions as possible within the time allowed.

You must mark your answers on the separate answer sheet. Do not write your answers in your test book.

PART 5

Directions: A word or phrase is missing in each of the sentences below. Four answer choices are given below each sentence. Select the best answer to complete the sentence. Then mark the letter (A), (B), (C), or (D) on your answer sheet.

就個人而言·Personally, I don't approve of her. 我不喜歡她
在他的推薦信裡頭
所有格+N.

101. After interviewing Miranda Song personally, the CEO ------- the position of Senior Creative Liaison specifically for her. */lɛ'zan/ adv. 特別地*
聯絡 *明確地*
(A) finished
(B) displayed *明確地* *具體地*
(C) hosted *v. 陳列·展出·誇*
(D) created *→He made a display of his learning.*
down, 拆除 誇耀自己有學問

102. Demolition of Tiger Stadium ------- due to *由於* safety concerns of neighboring property owners. *拆毀 鄰近的 房產擁有者*
(A) will have postponed
(B) is postponing *put postpone the evil hour*
(C) postpones *緩一緩必須做的*
(D) has been postponed *討厭的事*
n. 到場·出席 order 的·命令的
103. Attendance at the meeting is mandatory *強迫的* except for those employees with prior ------- . *除了那些有事先講的員工*
convert 改變
(A) adjustments *調整·校正*
(B) commitments *委任·託付·承諾 =change*
(C) announcements *=transform*
(D) conversions *改變·轉換*
被形容成
104. Homelessness is frequently described as an invisible problem, ------- its prevalence.
no + see
(A) while *無形的*
(B) until *n. 普遍 該的*
(C) despite *儘管·不管* *目前的*
(D) meanwhile *儘管遊民問題很普遍*
還是常被說成是無形的問題

105. In his letter of reference, Mr. Lopez expressed his ------- for Ms. Grant's ability to work well with others.
(A) admirable *adj. 可敬佩的·值得讚揚的*
(B) admiration *n.*
(C) admiring *adj. 仰慕的*
(D) admire *v. 欽佩·欣賞*
to 至 wonder

106. This Friday, all employees may depart two hours before closing ------- their manager requires them to stay.
(A) either *週五所有員工可以提早2小時離開*
(B) nor *除非經理要求要留下來*
(C) because
(D) unless *除非*

107. Located in Redwood Valley, California, Talent Tech Corp. develops ------- and hiring software. *對等連接詞*
(A) recruit *招募* *左右對等*
(B) recruiting *grow*
(C) recruitments
(D) recruiters *招聘人員*
根據公司政策·這種類的報告需要你
108. ------- company policy, all reports of this nature require the signature of your immediate supervisor.
(A) Instead of *目前的長官的簽名*
(B) According to
(C) Except *※nature n. 自然·紀模*
(D) Though *天性·本質·種類*

14

109. Economic data indicates that ------- no longer favor the Philippines as a priority destination.
(A) tourists
(B) tours
(C) tourism
(D) toured

110. The stories in Drew Cameron's latest collection are ------- the most imaginative narratives of his career.
(A) beside
(B) over
(C) among
(D) upon

111. Employees of Dyson Electronics receive substantial discounts when ------- shop at other stores in the Galleria Mall.
(A) theirs
(B) them
(C) their
(D) they

112. For many years, Orthodox International relied on a body within the company to ------- its products kosher.
(A) certify
(B) associate
(C) affect
(D) replace

113. Because electronic devices are easily -------, extra care must taken during their transport.
(A) damage
(B) damaging
(C) damaged
(D) damages

114. The merger will be finalized when ------- parties agree to the terms.
(A) both
(B) each
(C) so
(D) that

115. The real ------- of customer loyalty programs is the chance to turn good customers into great ones.
(A) value
(B) record
(C) amount
(D) tone

116. We are a modern thinking company who ------- to grow, with 19 locations worldwide.
(A) continual
(B) continued
(C) continue
(D) continually

117. As of January the property was still for sale, with ------- ongoing usage as an office complex.
(A) suggesting
(B) suggests
(C) suggest
(D) suggested

118. In 2004, the corporate headquarters were ------- to Ogden, Utah, to be closer to Hardcastle's mining operations.
(A) stored
(B) stayed
(C) based
(D) moved

119. Jefferson Nordic, producer of world-class skiing equipment, welcomes ------- ideas for improving our products.
(A) specific
(B) specify
(C) specifics
(D) specifically

120. Property management fees can be confusing, and it's difficult to determine what's appropriate and what's -------.
(A) as much
(B) as many
(C) too much
(D) too many

GO ON TO THE NEXT PAGE

15

121. At CashMaster, we monitor every transaction, 24/7, to help safeguard ------- fraudulent transactions and email phishing.
(A) since
(B) above
(C) against
(D) within

122. The JBN Elite Award recognizes executives who have not only ------- in sales but who are also brand ambassadors.
(A) excel
(B) excelled
(C) excellent
(D) excellence

123. Outpatient evaluations are ------- scheduled for two sessions of three hours each, although the duration of each session varies.
(A) almost
(B) right
(C) previously
(D) typically

124. The film was released ------- to video and was nominated for the Doomed Planet Award for "Worst Home Video Release."
(A) directing
(B) directly
(C) directs
(D) direct

125. It was then that Mr. Spicer announced he would ------- step down as CEO, effective immediately.
(A) conspicuously
(B) marginally
(C) regrettably
(D) intriguingly

126. The band's new album sold 2.5 million copies worldwide, bringing in a huge profit for Galaxy Records given the ------- production.
(A) inexpensive
(B) unhappy
(C) incomplete
(D) undecided

127. For the ------- majority of private equity investments, there is no listed public market; however, a secondary market is available.
(A) absolute
(B) tentative
(C) ethical
(D) vast

128. Several film directors have appeared in ------- films, sometimes with an uncredited cameo, or sometimes in a more major role.
(A) all
(B) others
(C) their own
(D) each one

129. Qualifying businesses are eligible for billions of dollars ------- tax incentives.
(A) for
(B) with
(C) at
(D) in

130. The area has seen a dramatic comeback as reinvestment has ------- once dilapidated homes into modern urban dwellings.
(A) is transforming
(B) transformed
(C) to transform
(D) transformation

PART 6

Directions: Read the texts that follow. A word, phrase, or sentence is missing in parts of the each text. Four answer choices are given below each of the text. Select the best answer to complete the text. Then mark the letter (A), (B), (C), or (D) on your answer sheet.

Questions 131-134 refer to the following letter.

April 8

Leslie Rosenbaum
Ebony Falcon Supply Co.
1478 46th Avenue
San Francisco, CA 94122

Dear Ms. Rosenbaum:

We are writing to dutifully inform you of a temporary ------- in our
131.
order fulfillment service.

On May 1, we will begin shipping orders from a new warehouse
in Berkeley. -------. The move will take up to two weeks, -------
132. **133.**
which time we may be unable to ship international orders.

------- any delays, please place your next order by April 15. If you
134.
have any questions, please don't hesitate to contact me.

Sincerely,
Otis Clemons
Cox-Franklin, Inc.
Director of Operations, Oakland

---

131. (A) improvement
(B) disruption
(C) explanation
(D) contribution

132. (A) Pirates have been spotted in the region
(B) Track the status of your order on the USPS Web site
(C) This will allow us to keep a wider variety of items in stock
(D) These will be available at a special price for a limited time

133. (A) instead of
(B) due to
(C) during
(D) below

134. (A) Avoids
(B) Avoided
(C) To avoid
(D) Having avoided

Questions 135-138 refer to the following e-mail.

From:	Bob Eiger, Vice-Chairman
To:	All Staff
Re:	Professional Development Seminar
Date:	Thursday, May 6

Dear Colleagues,

The first session of our professional development seminar will be held on May 27. The ------- lecture will be led by William Tremonte,
135.
manager of the country's largest hedge fund.

Mr. Tremonte ------- what established technology companies can
136.
learn from venture capitalists. Mr. Tremonte's talk is the only one in the series that tackles venture capitalism.

As you know, Mr. Tremonte is a mover and shaker in the financial world, so we hope all staff will be present.

Nevertheless, you must seek ------- your manager before attending.
138.

Thanks,

Bob Eiger

*lecture n. 授課. 演講. 訓斥   請不要對我說教
→ please don't lecture me.

leed-led-led
避險基金
最大的避險基金公司經理

創投資本家. 風險投資人
歷程

137.
具有號召力的人物

Venture n. 冒險. 投資活動 capitalism 資本主義   →創投
所有員工都參加

137 (A)當學生的時候. 他發表了一篇文章在一本很有名望的財政經濟雜誌上
(B)其他的會處理各種主題, 包括了品牌拓展和客戶關係
(C) 很多避險基金都是私底下擁有的.
(D) 專業的發展研習會在科技領域裡越來越受歡迎

revise 修正
135. (A) revised
B (B) opening + ceremony 開幕式
    (C) final   night   首映日
    (D) wholly   transaction 閉市
                 speech 閉幕詞

136. (A) discussed
B (B) will discuss
    (C) has discussed
    (D) will have discussed

有名望的
137. (A) As a student, Mr. Tremonte published an
        article in a prestigious financial magazine
B   (B) The rest will deal with various other topics,
        including branding and customer relations
    (C) Many large hedge funds are privately owned
    (D) Professional development seminars are
        gaining popularity in the field of technology

approval n. 贊同. 許可
approve v. 贊同. 同意

138. (A) approving
C   (B) who approves
    (C) the approval of
    (D) having approved

approving adj. 贊同的
嘉許的

18

BMTA Public Updates Announced

The Baltimore Metropolitan Transit Authority will ------- a series of service
139.

updates to the public at four meetings at the end of March. -------.
140.

The proposed updates include a new Saturday Penn Station-Midtown route, a new east side flex zone, revised route identification and route adjustments that would create more direct service and one-seat rides.

The meetings ------- at the following times:
141.

March 28 – Baltimore Public Library, 1515 SW 10th Street, Barre Circle
    3:00–5:00 p.m.

March 29 – Quincy Courthouse, 820 SE Quincy Lane
    7:00–9:00 a.m.

March 30 – Garfield Community Center, 1600 NE Rickshaw Road
    11:00 a.m.–1:00 p.m.

March 31 – Avondale East, 455 SE Eutaw Park Blvd.
    6:00–8:00 p.m.

All feedback will ------- the Baltimore Metro Board of Directors for action
142.
on April 20.

139. (A) present
     (B) presenting
     (C) presenter
     (D) presentation

140. (A) The Penn Station-Midtown Line was finished six weeks ahead of schedule
     (B) The service changes are designed to modernize Baltimore transit
     (C) The commission chair will run for mayor next year
     (D) The TMTA has decided to hold monthly meetings

141. (A) did occur
     (B) will occur
     (C) occurring
     (D) occurred

142. (A) reminded to
     (B) be considered by
     (C) have persuaded
     (D) take notice at

GO ON TO THE NEXT PAGE.

From:	wesglavin@royalfarms.com
To:	lougrist@jerseyshorealpacas.com
Re:	Alpacas
Date:	June 12

Dear Mr. Grist,

I represent Royal Farms, one of the largest free-range chicken growers in the mid-Atlantic. Our farm is now in the process of -------- to fresh-range turkeys. We are extremely interested in acquiring a few alpacas to help guard and tend the flocks. Having learned about this -------- at the Maryland State Fair, we contacted the Mid-Atlantic **143.**

144.
Alpaca Association, which recommended your breeding program to us. On your Web site, it appears you -------- lease alpacas, but do not

145.
sell them. Initially, we would be interested in buying at least one pair of animals. --------. In the meantime, do you offer tours of your alpaca

146.
farm?

I look forward to hearing from you.

Sincerely,
Wes Glavin
Royal Farms

143. (A) expanding
(B) expanded
(C) expands
(D) expand

144. (A) formula
(B) method
(C) ability
(D) variety

145. (A) currently
(B) patiently
(C) quietly
(D) eventually

146. (A) However, we would be interested in more in the future
(B) If you do, please visit our Web site for more information on our offer
(C) Our farm has been family-owned for over 50 years
(D) Unfortunately, they are no longer in demand at this point

PART 7

Directions: In this part you will read a selection of texts, such as magazine and newspaper articles, e-mails, and instant messages. Each text or set of texts is followed by several questions. Select the best answer for each question and mark the letter (A), (B), (C), or (D) on your answer sheet.

Questions 147-148 refer to the following customer review.

= praising
A flattering = complimentary
討人喜歡的 = favourable
媚人的
奉承的 = He likes to make flattering remarks. 奉承的話

SHOE REVIEWS.COM

https://www.shoereviews.com/sampsonmetrowalkers

Sampson Metro Walkers

⭐☆☆☆☆ (1 out of 5 stars / 2.73 average rating)

Submitted by user: Richard Kirby

Compromise
舒適度
v.妥協.讓步
第一優先順位
科學與工業博物館

I spend eight hours a day leading tours at the Museum of Science and Industry, so comfort is always my number one priority when selecting shoes. However, I refuse to compromise on style. I've tried many brands of shoes, but I've never found any that I'm completely happy with. They're either unflattering or end up hurting my feet. I was so happy when I discovered the Sampson Metro Walkers because they are both comfortable and stylish. Unfortunately, I've only had them three weeks and the soles have almost completely worn through. I really need something that can hold up to consistent use for at least a year. Needless to say, I will not be buying them again.

拒絕
黯淡 不討喜的
舒服 又 好看
鞋底
wear through 磨破.損壞
支撐.延誤 The storm held us up.
放晴: It will hold up this afternoon.
更不用說 不言而喻

consistent
始終如一的 a consistent standard
前後一致的 to be consistent with sth → His behavior is consistent with his teaching.

147. What is suggested about Mr. Kirby?
D (A) His shoe size is not common. 腳尺寸不常見
   (B) He works in a shoe repair shop. 修鞋店
   (C) He recently moved to a new city. 搬到新城市
   (D) His job requires a lot of walking. 需要走很多路

148. What did Mr. Kirby dislike about Sampson Metro Walkers?
D (A) Their unattractive style. 不好看
   (B) Their poor fit on his feet. 不合腳了
   (C) Their expensive price. 價格高
   (D) Their lack of durability. 耐久性不高
   durable adj. 耐用的, 持久的

GO ON TO THE NEXT PAGE.

JEFFERS LANDSCAPING

RATED #1 LANDSCAPER
IN SILVER LAKE
•
FULLY BONDED
BETTER BUSINESS BUREAU™
APPROVED

Our Service

We provide the highest quality landscaping services in Silver Lake. Whether you've got a small back yard or acres of land, Pinnacle provides access to landscaping and maintenance solutions that suit your needs. We specialize in personalized landscape designs and upkeep with an exceptional eye for detail. And unlike our competitors, Pinnacle offers year-round maintenance plans for leaf collection and snow removal.

End of Summer Promo

$50 off with the purchase of an annual maintenance plan

Jeffers Landscaping
Silver Lake
545-1290

149. What is indicated about Jeffers Landscaping?
(A) Its employees have experience installing fences.
(B) It is seeking to hire new landscaping professionals.
(C) It operates throughout the year.
(D) It offers lower prices than its competitors.

150. What is NOT offered by Jeffers Landscaping?
(A) Snow removal.
(B) Recycling services.
(C) Landscape design.
(D) Leaf collection.

22

From:	Fiona Germaine <f.germaine@webfoot.com>
To:	Cole Minn <c.minn@webfoot.com>
Re:	Grady Globetrotter
Date:	April 4

Cole,

I have some great news to share with you! I've been offered a chance work on Grady Globetrotter's new photography Web site, and I'd like you to be involved. Ideally, they would like it to be completed by the end of this month, which doesn't give us a lot of time.

The editor-in-chief, Grady Kuo, has very specific preferences about colors, fonts, layout, and image sizes, which he just sent to me. His e-mail is: g_kuo@gradyimages.com. Drop him a note so we are both up to speed on what he has in mind.

I would also like you to join me on a quick conference call with him tomorrow afternoon at 4:30 so we can go over some of these details. The number is 503-407-2319, and use conference code 78656 to join the call.

Fiona

151. What news does Ms. Germaine share?

(A) She will be attending a trade show.
(B) She will be hiring a photographer.
(C) She has been given a new project.
(D) She has deleted an account.

152. What topic will be discussed during the conference call?

(A) Design elements
(B) Payment specifications
(C) Marketing strategies.
(D) Severance packages.

GO ON TO THE NEXT PAGE.

[1:45 PM] Beth Underwood

Buddy, have you completed section seven of the training module yet? I need to format it.

訓練模組第7部分你完成了沒有 我要把它們格式化了.

[1:46 PM] Buddy Stoggs

我只要拿到修正(審查)過的安全方針部分就可以完成

It will be finished as soon as I get the revised safety guidelines from Jennifer Simpson. I'm expecting her to have them ready soon.

從Jennifer那裡

我希望(期待)她快點把它們用好。

[1:47 PM] Beth Underwood

當你在等的時候, 可以把剩下的先寄給我嗎 我答應Grant今天下班前會給他最後的草稿.

While you're waiting, could you please send me the rest of it? I promised Grant Evans I'd get the final draft to him by the end of the day.

[1:46 PM] Buddy Stoggs

佔位符(做記號的小貼紙)

OK. I'll put in a placeholder for the guidelines so we'll all remember where in the training session we're planning to list them.

訓練活動 *我們預計(計劃)列的地方*

[1:47 PM] Beth Underwood

*await v. long-awaited 期待已久的
→ Death awaits all men. 人總有一死

That'll work.

被要求做什麼?

153. What has Ms. Simpson been asked to do? *更新一些素材.*

(A) Update some materials. *安排客戶會議*

(B) Schedule a client meeting.

(C) Meet with Mr. Stoggs.

(D) Send a reminder to Ms. Underwood. *寄送提醒*

同意訓練模組

154. At 1:50 P.M., what does Ms. Underwood most likely mean when she writes, "That works"? *等候.期待.等待* *辭職*

(A) She will await Ms. Schrote's resignation.

(B) She agrees to Mr. Stoggs's suggestion.

(C) She has approved the training module.

(D) She believes Mr. Evans can complete his work on time.

Chet Atkins Guitar Museum ✕

https//:www.cagm.com/admission

Admission	
Child (under 12)	
	$8.95
Adult	
	$14.95
Senior Citizen (65 and up)	
	$10.95

For only $199.95, you can enjoy:
• Free admission for one year
• 10% off at the Museum Cafe and the Atkins Theater
• Free parking
• 5 one-day guest passes

NEW !!! Become a Chet Atkins Guitar Museum Patron and save!

YES! I want to be a CAGM Patron	Qty.
	1
CAGM Patron	
	$199.95

Provide the following payment and contact information to become a CAGM *Patron*.

Name:

Lester Collingsworth

E-mail:

les.collinsworth@mailserve.com

Address:

10957 Beall Road

City/State/Zip:

Rockville, MD 20850

Payment method:

Credit card ▼

SUBMIT

Once your order is successfully submitted, your proof of purchase will be sent to the e-mail address provided above. Please print this document and present it at the Chet Atkins Guitar Museum Atkins Theater box office to receive your Patron card.

155. How much will Mr. Collingsworth pay?
(A) $8.95.
(B) $10.95.
(C) $14.95.
(D) $199.95.

156. What is Mr. Collingsworth directed to do?
(A) Accept an application form.
(B) Bring his receipt to the box office.
(C) Enter an access code.
(D) Reply to an e-mail message.

157. What is NOT mentioned as a benefit available to Mr. Collingsworth?
(A) Guest passes.
(B) Free parking.
(C) Low rates on classes.
(D) A discount on food.

GO ON TO THE NEXT PAGE.

Questions 158-160 refer to the following e-mail.

From:	Digital Station <orders@digitaldepot.com>
To:	Richard Lonz <swineflu99@retrogroup.com>
Re:	Order 89324-09
Date:	December 8

| Order 89324-09 | Customer: LONZ, Richard | Date: December 8 |

Thank you for your order placed today at 11:36 a.m. through Digital Depot's online store for the following items:

(1)	Grooves HD Headphones
(2)	London Symphony in Concert (Blu-Ray disc)
(3)	25 Easy Vegan Recipes (e-book format)

digitaldepot

Unfortunately, we are unable to process your order because the credit card you had previously registered in our system has expired. However, your order will remain active for the next two weeks. So that we might still process your order, please update your payment information on our Web site at your earliest convenience. We also accept checks and money orders. Please note that if no payment is received by December 22, your order will be canceled.

Digital Depot Customer Service Center

---

158. Why was the e-mail sent?
(A) To report difficulty in processing a payment.
(B) To explain that items are no longer available.
(C) To inquire about shipping preferences.
(D) To provide an estimated delivery date.

159. What is NOT indicated about Mr. Lonz's order?
(A) It was submitted early in the day.
(B) It must be paid for within two weeks.
(C) It included recorded music.
(D) It will be delivered by December 22.

160. What is Mr. Lonz asked to do?
(A) Update his payment information.
(B) Reply to the e-mail.
(C) Choose different items.
(D) Provide his mailing address.

From:	Daisy Nimitrov <dnimitrov@genmail.com>
To:	Terry Trevans <strevans@sierrajet.com>
Re:	In-flight meal 機內餐
Date:	October 23

Dear Ms. Nimitrov,

Thank you for your e-mail. —[1]—.

We at Sierra Jetways are sorry that we were unable to accommodate your special meal request during your flight to Los Angeles International Airport.

To compensate for our error, we would like to offer a **credit of 7,500 miles** to your frequent-flyer account, bringing your total to 34,000 miles. —[2]—.

Please inform us of your preference by replying to this e-mail. You may also contact me at the number below. —[3]—.

Again, we apologize for the inconvenience. We hope that you will continue to choose Sierra Jetways for your future travel needs. —[4]—.

Terry Trevans
Customer Service Manager
Sierra Jetways
800-449-0099 ext. 2874

*(handwritten annotations present: ③向...提供 The bank will accommodate him with a loan. ②通融; /sɪˈɛrə/ n.鋸狀山脈; 不能夠 v.符合/供應; 補償; 錯誤; 提供; 常飛者戶頭; 喜好; 回覆; 抱歉造成您的不方便; 希望未來您有飛行需求時還是能繼續選擇我們航空公司; *voucher 票 /vautʃɚ/ gift voucher 禮券 phone voucher 手機充值卡)*

---

161. What is the purpose of the e-mail?
- (A) To provide details about an upcoming business trip.
- (B) To advertise a promotion on Sierra Jetways flights.
- (C) To offer compensation to a dissatisfied customer.
- (D) To update information about in-flight meal option.

162. What is suggested about Ms. Nimitrov?
- (A) She requested a specific seat on her flight.
- (B) She bought her most recent ticket at a discount.
- (C) She will inform the airline about her meal preference.
- (D) She often travels with Sierra Jetways.

163. In which of the positions marked [1], [2], [3], and [4] does the following sentence best belong?
"You also have the option of accepting a voucher for $150 USD for an upcoming flight with Sierra Jetways or any of our partner airlines."
- (A) [1].
- (B) [2].
- (C) [3].
- (D) [4].

GO ON TO THE NEXT PAGE.

Naperville Business Beat:
SCUPPY'S BRINGS BACK PRINT CATALOG

(July 29)—After ceasing print production of its merchandise catalogs several years ago, Scuppy's has decided to bring them back, the store announced this week.

A questionnaire sent to Scuppy's customers last year revealed that the majority favored the return of the paper catalog. Stuart O'Shea, a spokesperson for the store, explained that many customers prefer to browse through an actual hard-copy catalog, even if they later order an item online.

He found that shoppers typically purchase products for the home from the catalog. Unlike their original catalog, which contained over 90 percent of their store merchandise, the new catalog will focus mainly on these items and give limited space to merchandise ordered a little less frequently, such as apparel items.

Media specialist Gordon Heaple noted that print catalogs will serve a purpose in the digital age. "Sometimes it's easier to find the product you want by flipping through real pages," she remarked, "whereas retail Web sites are sometimes difficult to navigate."

According to Mr. O'Shea, Scuppy's new print catalog is scheduled to appear twice this year. It will be mailed to customers and distributed in stores. It will also be available for downloading on Scuppy's Web site.

Scuppy's began as a children's toy store in Darien. Over its 80-year history, it moved to Naperville and expanded into a department store selling a full array of high-quality goods. It boasts a devoted following throughout suburban Chicago, with many customers willing to travel several hours to shop there.

- *by Thad Strock*

164. What is the purpose of the article?
(A) To profile a local company executive.
(B) To report on a business expansion.
(C) To introduce a new Web site.
(D) To announce the return of a publication.

165. The word "noted" in paragraph 4, line 2, is closest in meaning to
(A) went down.
(B) drew.
(C) recorded.
(D) pointed out.

166. According to the article, what did Scuppy's do last year?
(A) It started to offer children's toys.
(B) It developed a new advertising campaign.
(C) It surveyed its customers.
(D) It relocated its headquarters.

167. What is suggested about Scuppy's?
(A) It has acquired many loyal customers.
(B) It is a popular tourist destination.
(C) It sells mainly children's goods.
(D) It has two store locations.

STUDY: LEARNING A FOREIGN LANGUAGE IMPROVES LISTENING SKILLS

By Rondell Forsythe

DETROIT. (August 5)—A new study has revealed that learning to speak a foreign language can greatly improve listening skills. – [1] –.

The study, "Hearing Vs. Listening: The Positive Auditory Effects of Foreign Language Acquisition," consisted of observations, interviews, and a series of auditory tests for its 1,000 participants. – [2] –. Fifty participants in the study (adults as well as children) were assigned foreign languages and provided with classes to learn to speak those languages at a basic to an intermediate level over a two-year time frame. – [3] –.

The results of the study showed that those individuals who learned to speak a new language were able to distinguish sounds and pitches more accurately after two years of study. The other participants showed little, if any, improvement. "Learning to speak a foreign language helps a person to develop a strong sense of sound differentiation," explains Jacob Wolfe, one of the study's head researchers. "– [4] –. It is because foreign languages in particular challenge our patterns of expression, I believe we are seeing these enhanced auditory abilities in some participants."

GO ON TO THE NEXT PAGE.

29

168. What is the topic of the recently published study? 最近出版的研究主題是

C

(A) How age affects the ability to 什麼
learn a foreign language.

(B) How learning in a group affects
language <u>acquisition</u>. 獲得

(C) How learning a new language
affects listening ability. 聽力技巧(能力)

(D) How listening to foreign music
affects a person's <u>mood</u>. 心情

169. Who is Mr. Wolfe?

D

(A) A news reporter. 新聞播報員
(B) A language coach. 語言教練
(C) A study participant. 研究參與者
(D) A leader of a study. 研究領導者

170. In which of the positions marked [1], [2], [3], and [4] does the following sentence best belong?

C

"The other 500 did not learn a foreign language."

(A) [1].
(B) [2].
(C) [3].
(D) [4].

對於「參加測試者」何者指示是對?

171. What is indicated about the participants in the study? 被要求

D

(A) All of them were required to learn a foreign language.

(B) Some of them spoke at an advanced level. 口說是進階等級

(C) Only 500 of them had to complete an interview. 完成一場面試

(D) Some of them learned a new language for two years.

學了兩年新語言

---

168. (A) 年齡如何可影響 學習語言的能力

(B) 從團體中學習對語言獲取的影響

(C) 學習新語言如何影響聽力能力

(D) 聽外文音樂如何影響一個人的心情

﹡<u>affect</u>   v. ① 影響
to make   ② 假裝 He affected not to see her.
/əˈfɛkt/   ③ 愛用 She affects old toys.

effect   n. ① 結果
/ɪˈfɛkt/   ② 作用 + on/upon
   ③ 意義、要旨: I said a few words to the effect that ~

v. 實現,達到目的 He effected several important
   完成幾項重要的改革   changes.

Questions 172-175 refer to the following online chat discussion.

adj. 編輯的. 社論的   n. 社論. (電台.電視的) 重要評論

Jill Law [9:52 A.M.]

Hi Trent and Byron. I have some unfortunate news about the assistant editorial position. Two of the three finalists for the job backed out before their scheduled second interviews next week.

不幸的   消息   關於   助理編輯的 職位
ㄐㄧ ㄢ ㄒㄩㄢ
3個參加決選的人當中有兩個人 在他們被安排參加下週第二輪面試前退出了. (back out)

Byron Ezra [9:55 A.M.]

Why does this keep happening to our department? This also happened the last time, when Trent was hired. Is the benefits package a problem?

為何我們部門一直發生這種事?
上次也這樣了
是我們公司的福利方案出問題了嗎

Trent Chambers [9:54 A.M.]

Who is left?

go with ①同意②相配 Do you think the hat go with my new dress?
③跟~約會 He goes with the girl every week.

Jill Law [9:57 A.M.]

The remaining candidate is Crystal Scott. She's the only one who brought her portfolio to the interview, remember? That work was impressive. She has all the necessary qualifications, including a master's degree in journalism from Emerson. Should we look for new candidates or go with Ms. Scott?

adj 剩下的   候選人   是   她是唯一一個有帶她的檔案來面試的人
計事帳   那個work讓人印象深刻
必要的   資格(條件)   碩士學位
我們應該找新的候選人還是選擇Scott小姐呢?

Trent Chambers [9:59 A.M.]

Byron, the benefits package is comparable to what other companies are offering. The problem is we take too long to decide whom to hire. Candidates are accepting other job offers while we're still making up our minds.

比得上的
當我們還在下定決心(做決定)時. 候選人正在接受別的工作了

Jill Law [10:01 A.M.]

I couldn't have said it better myself.

use to wholeheartedly agree with somebody else's remark. 非常同意別人說的話

Byron Ezra [10:02 A.M.]

Let's offer a contract to Ms. Scott then. She looks good on paper, and she did a great job in her initial interview.

那麼我們就給他個合約吧?   她書面資料看起來不錯, 而且她
起初的面試表現的不錯.
adj 開始的. 最初的

GO ON TO THE NEXT PAGE.

172. What is true about the position? 職位發还何者

D   (A) It <u>attracted</u> only two applicants. 只吸引 兩位申請者

為真
人

     (B) It has <u>been advertised</u> for two months. 已經廣告2個月了

     (C) It needs to <u>be filled</u> by next week. 下週前要達標

     (D) It requires a degree in <u>journalism</u>. 需要新聞相關文憑

173. At 9:01 A.M., what does Ms. Law most likely mean when she writes, "I couldn't have said it better myself"?

C

他的工作行程 和他同事的行程 不一樣

     (A) She wants to interview other candidates. 想面試其他候選人

     (B) She thinks that Ms. Scott will accept the offer. 接受這個好意(職位)

     (C) She believes that the hiring process is too slow. 雇用過程太慢

     (D) She agrees that the salary needs to be raised. 薪水要調高

174. What is suggested about Mr. Chambers?

D

     (A) He schedules all interviews for the department. 他為部門主排所有面試

     (B) He has a work schedule different from that of his colleagues.

     (C) He led the job interview with Ms. Scott.

     (D) He is the newest member of the department. 部門最新的員工

175. What did Ms. Law like about Ms. Scott? 對於問題的解決方法

B

     (A) Her solution to a problem.

     (B) Her previous work. 之前的表現

     (C) Her series of questions.

     (D) Her research on the company. 她對公司的研究

※ 拉丁字源開頭的字，比較正式
re, ex, con

ask for	=	request	find out	= enquire
go back	=	return	move toward	= approach
get back	=	regain	put up with	= tolerate
look back	=	review	refer to	= consult 提及
come up to	=	reach	make sure of	= ensure
deal with	=	manage	give in	= yield
lead to	=	cause	get away	= escape
look for	=	seek	throw away	= discard
look into	=	investigate		
think about	=	consider		
go ahead	=	proceed		

From:	Grant Thornton, Deputy Director
To:	All Los Angeles Museum of Modern Art staff
Re:	Post-Modern Exhibition
Date:	May 23

✉ Review Quotes (PDF) 18.8k

Dear LAMOMA Staff,

You have my sincere gratitude for your work on the recent "Post-Modern Los Angeles" exhibition. It was warmly received by critics, scholars, and other art professionals. Attached is a selection of review quotes attesting to the show's success. *California Today* called the show "a brilliant gem of L.A.'s Post-Modern movement." Quite surprisingly, it was rated 10 out of 10 by L.A.'s most outspoken critic, Yasuhiro Sakei, an unprecedented achievement.

Because of the exhibition's success, the LAMOMA Board of Trustees has voted to fund an upgrade to our museum's Sculpture Atrium. Thus, we can continue to curate the most exceptional new works of the West Coast art scene. Renovations to the Atrium will commence early next year.

Over the past two weeks, our new chief curator, Amanda Leiber, has been planning the summer exhibition schedule with me. Please join us for an all-staff meeting on April 16 in Conference Room B at 9:45 a.m. Amanda will introduce herself and present our ideas.

Keep up the great work!

Grant Thornton

GO ON TO THE NEXT PAGE.

"Both a breathtaking wonder and a sublime treat."

—Dasmarinas Savoy, Art Critic, *Los Angeles Tribune*

"If you see one show this year, make sure it's this one."

—Anthony Hicks, *Bel-Air Journal of Design*

"A brilliant gem of L.A.'s post-modern movement."

—Delphine Abebe, *California Today*

10/10. In fact, if I could say 11/10, I would."

—Yasuhiro Sakei, *Cutting Edge L.A.*

"The kind of exhibition that inspires and invigorates."

—Joe Pizzini, *Downtown*

176. What is the purpose of the e-mail?
(A) To notify personnel about a cancelled exhibition.
(B) To encourage workers to improve their skills.
(C) To advise staff about a job opening.
(D) To praise employees for their work.

177. What does Mr. Thornton ask recipients of the e-mail to do?
(A) Work extra hours.
(B) Complete a questionnaire.
(C) Attend a meeting.
(D) Write a review.

178. What reviewer's rating particularly pleases Mr. Thornton?
(A) Ms. Savoy's.
(B) Mr. Hicks's.
(C) Mr. Sakei's.
(D) Mr. Pizzini's.

179. For what publication does Mr. Pizzini write?
(A) Downtown.
(B) Los Angeles Tribune.
(C) Bel-Air Journal of Design.
(D) Cutting Edge L.A.

180. Who is Ms. Leiber?
(A) A senior curator.
(B) A deputy director.
(C) An acclaimed artist.
(D) An art critic.

From:	thomas_foy@mailbox.com
To:	customerservice@lonestarsports.com
Re:	Purchase Order 4328 訂單編號
Date:	June 13

✉ T. Foy Bank Statement (PDF) 23.6k

Dear Customer Service,

買了一雙 美維吉尼亞州-阿靈頓

On May 28, I purchased a pair of Maxx Shock Z28 running shoes at the Lone Star Sports' Arlington location. I paid for the purchase with my <u>debit card</u>. I have been pleased with the shoes and was satisfied with the price and the quality of the item.

滿足(意) 戶頭有多.刷多 result His failure resulted largely
銀行帳單   v.產生發生 from his laziness.

When I received my bank statement, however, I noticed that I had been charged twice. I called the Arlington store to resolve the problem. The clerk said that there was a company-wide system problem that day, which <u>resulted in</u> several <u>duplicate charges</u>. She told me to e-mail customer service, and a representative would promptly <u>handle</u> the issue and reimburse me accordingly.

系統問題 全公司的 adj.複製的
趨 n.複製品.副本
adv.敘述地 處理 問題 補償

I have attached my bank statement for your reference.

adv.①相應地 prompt
Sincerely, ②於是 adj. He is prompt in paying the rent 迅速的
Thomas Foy =thus adv. They started at 7:00 prompt. 正(時間)

*He was too sick =hence v.促使 His curiosity prompted him to
to stay. =therefore 激起 ask questions.
Accordingly, As it is, n.提詞 to give sb. a prompt
Consequently, As a result,
Thus, Subsequently, we send him home.
Hence,
Therefore,
In that case,

GO ON TO THE NEXT PAGE.

益單子補充整理
1. assignment 分配工作
2. bulletin 公報、告示、定期報告書
3. calculator 計算機
4. carbon copy 副本
5. extension 分機
6. intercom 對講機
7. operator 接線生
8. printed matter 印刷品
電子薪水轉帳

COMMENTS Statement period: May 1 – May 30

Date: June 1
STATEMENT # 98421
BILL TO
Thomas Foy
2389 Walkerton Street,
Dallas, Texas 54383
Customer ID FNB92232

Date	Description	Balance	Amount
May 5	Electronic Salary Transfer - Jersey Construction Co.	$16,829.01	+$7,023.33
May 11	Derby Market, Dallas, TX	$16,794.36	-$34.65
May 15	Fort Worth Florist, Ft. Worth, TX	$16,694.36	-$100.00
May 16	Derby Market, Dallas, TX	$16,459.39	-$234.97
May 28	Lone Star Sports, Arlington, TX	$16,337.72	-$121.67
May 28	Lone Star Sports, Arlington, TC	$16,216.05	-$121.67

Current	1-30 Days Past Due	31-60 Days Past Due	61-90 Days Past Due	Over 90 Days Past Due	Ending balance
n/a	n/a	n/a	n/a		$16,216.05

9. receptionist 接待員
10. shorthand 速記(法)
11. stardy 遲緩、遲到的
12. typist 打頭
13. xerox /ˈzɪræks/ 影印
14. attendance 出席人數
15. directory 人名住址等
16. duplicate 副本
17. filing 歸檔

181. In the e-mail, the word "handle" is closest in meaning to
C
(A) create. 創造
(B) deliver. 運送
(C) manage 管理
(D) hold. 把持

182. When did Mr. Foy probably purchase flowers?
C
(A) On May 5.
(B) On May 11.
(C) On May 15.
(D) On May 28.

183. For what type of company does Mr. Foy most likely work? 建設公司
A
(A) A construction company.
(B) A law firm. 法律公司
(C) A local bank. 當地銀行
(D) A furniture store. 家俱行

184. What does the e-mail indicate about Mr. Foy?
A
(A) He likes the shoes he purchased.
(B) He has visited the Arlington location several times since February. 高興的、滿意的
(C) He is not pleased with the return policy at Lone Star Sports.
對於退貨政策不滿意
(D) He is a long-distance runner.
是個長距離賽跑者

185. What amount does Mr. Foy expect to be refunded? 多少金額預計被退還
C
(A) $34.65.
(B) $100.00.
(C) $121.67.
(D) $234.97.

From:	Katrina Cline <kcline@russiantearoom.com>
To:	Chad Loomer <jloomer@russiantearoom.com>
Re:	Latest Update
Date:	July 17

Hello Chad,

My father just called to inform me that he has decided to have the restaurant renovated. As the on-site management team, the two of us will be the points of contact for the workers who will complete the project. As a first step, I would like to ask you to identify some potential companies to do the work. Please begin looking into this as soon as possible and provide me with an update by July 31.

From:	Buddy Covington <bcovington@csrdesign.com>
To:	Katrina Cline <kcline@russiantearoom.com>
Re:	Project
Date:	August 7

Dear Ms. Cline,

On behalf of the team at Covington & Sons Restaurant Design, we are pleased that we have been selected for the Russian Tea Room's remodeling project. As I discussed with your assistant by telephone yesterday, we will provide a project supervisor and a designer who will be devoted to helping you create just the right look for your restaurant. We work with local wholesalers to offer you a wide selection of products, including paint, furniture, light fixtures and flooring, all within the restaurant's budget. We expect to complete the project by September 1.

We can discuss this information in more detail at our meeting on August 14.

Sincerely,
Buddy Covington
Covington and Sons Restaurant Design

GO ON TO THE NEXT PAGE

HOME | REVIEW | CONTACT | ABOUT

SEPTEMBER 15 - CHANGES AT THE RUSSIAN TEA ROOM
by Landon Yates

During the first week of September, I dined two nights at the Russian Tearoom Restaurant while attending a business meeting. Overall, the food is exactly the same – delicious! However, it looks better than it did the last time I visited. The hostess desk is now well-lit and inviting, and the worn vinyl armchairs in the bar and lounge area have been replaced by cozy plush sofas. The restaurant has a tasteful color scheme that is carried out throughout the dining rooms. It is a little disappointing to see a family-owned restaurant decide on such a corporate look, but the renovations to the building exterior were not yet complete. I hope they keep at least some of the charming touches that make it special, such as the unique dragonfly mosaic around the entranceway. Ultimately, what keeps people coming back is the food.

Done | Internet

186. Why was first e-mail sent?
- (A) To announce a merger.
- (B) To offer a suggestion.
- (C) To assign a task.
- (D) To update a schedule.

187. What is Mr. Yates unhappy about?
- (A) The bar lounge furniture is uncomfortable.
- (B) The reception area is too brightly lit.
- (C) The restaurant has lost some of its charm.
- (D) The restaurant was bought by a large corporation.

188. Who most likely did Mr. Covington talk to on August 6?
- (A) Mr. Loomer.
- (B) Mr. Yates.
- (C) Ms. Cline.
- (D) Mr. Cline.

189. What is suggested about the renovation?
- (A) It cost more than anticipated.
- (B) It included the addition of meeting rooms.
- (C) It has caused an increase in reservations.
- (D) It was not completed on schedule.

190. What does Mr. Covington offer Ms. Cline in his e-mail to her?
- (A) To make decisions rapidly with the vendors.
- (B) To provide dedicated staff members for the project.
- (C) To send her weekly memos on the status of the project.
- (D) To pay a penalty if the project is finished late.

烹飪的 藝術品 (技術)

SUSCA Spencer University School of Culinary Arts

808 Edgewater Boulevard - Gaithersburg, Maryland 24977

款待 鼓勵招待 尖端

Register now for classes designed to help you develop cutting-edge food preparation and hospitality skills. All classes are taught by instructors with <u>extensive</u> 大量的 廣泛的 professional experience and meet for fifteen weeks starting in either the second week of February or in the second week of September. 所有課程都是由有大量經驗的 專業老師教授，要會面15 週,可以從二月第二週或是 9月第二週開始。

BASIC KITCHEN ACCOUNTING

Instructor: Arlene Raphael

磨利 (變尖)

Sharpen your administration skills by managing inventory, food costs, and labor expenses.

Meeting times: Monday and Wednesday, 7:15—9:00 P.M.

PROFESSIONAL DINING SERVICE

Instructor: Takeshi Harada

檔成要素 和架構 服務規則

→ /ɛtɪkɛt/
禮節. 禮儀

Learn the basic components and structure of dining service rules and etiquette.

Meeting time: Tuesday, 7:15—9:00 P.M.

= manners

公共衛生. 環境衛生 小要素.要點

FOOD SANITATION ESSENTIALS

= social code
= decencies

Instructor: Cameron Vegas

= formalities

Learn the proper food handling and storage techniques, as well as government regulations

Meeting time: Thursday, 7:15—9:00 P.M.

BAKING BASICS

Instructor: N'dela Odimpi

Take your cooking skills to the next level by learning how to bake.

Meeting times: Friday, 7:15—9:30 P.M.

可以單獨上課或是多人一起報註課 捆,捲 / (b)大批,大量

Note: Classes may be taken individually or bundled. The American Culinary Certification (Level II) requires participants to successfully complete all four classes in the program. 要拿到證照,參加者要成功完成所有4堂課程

GO ON TO THE NEXT PAGE.

From:	bmxavier@scootmail.com
To:	araphael@susca.edu
Re:	Job Reference
Date:	November 4

✉ Xavier resume and job description (PDF) 23.6K

Dear Ms. Raphael,

apply for 申請

I am applying for a position at Ida's Jack Steakhouse and 牛排館
would like to know if I may use you as a reference since 由於
我是否可以用你的6課當作推薦資料
你的課和這份工作表有關聯
your class was most relevant to the job. Please let me know
嗎你一有空就告訴我
at your earliest convenience. I would like to submit my
申請表   這週結束之前   需要列出我的推薦信在線上
我想要繳交
application by the end of this week and need to include my
申請表裡
references in the online application. I have attached a
附上一個文件讓你看   習含工作描述和我的履歷
document for you to review, it includes both the job
description and my resume. ——→ ≠ resume
ɛ ju e   /rɪˈzjum/   恢復；重新開始
推薦(教學)
Thank you again for your instruction. I enjoyed being in
your class.

多益單字補充
1 in-tray 待處理文件盒
Barry Monroe Xavier
2 out-tray 已處理文件盒
11 authorize 授權
12 bonus 紅利津貼   3 partition 分隔物(如牆壁)
13 capability 能力.潛能 4. postage 郵費
14 collaboration 合作 5. punctuality 準時.守時
15 eligible 合格的   6. shift 輪班.換班
16 lay off 解雇   7. strike 罷工
17 permanent 永久的   8. work force 工作人員.勞動人口
18 recruit 招募
19 amateur 外行.業餘者 9. allocate 撥出.分配.配置
20 appoint 任命.指定   10. applicant 申請人

40

From:	araphael@susca.edu
To:	bmxavier@scootmail.com
Re:	Job Reference
Date:	November 4

Hi Mr. Xavier,

I would be happy to serve as a reference. You picked up the information presented in our class very quickly, so I think you'll be a good fit for a fast-paced environment like Ida's Jack. I reviewed your resume and just wanted to remind you that the class was one that <u>contributes to</u> a certificate. You completed the program in June, so you should <u>indicate</u> that you earned a Level II ACF certification.

Best wishes!
Arlene Raphael, SUSCA Instructor

191. What is stated about all of the listed classes?
(A) They are designed specifically for restaurant owners.
(B) They are offered twice a year.
(C) They must be taken together.
(D) They focus on how to start a business.

192. What is suggested about Mr. Xavier?
(A) He is a candidate for a job at SUSCA.
(B) He failed Ms. Raphael's class.
(C) He completed four classes at SUSCA.
(D) He earned a certificate in April.

193. What about Mr. Xavier most impressed Ms. Raphael?
(A) His resume.
(B) His certifications.
(C) His learning speed.
(D) His test scores.

194. Who most likely has experience in a bakery?
(A) Mr. Vegas.
(B) Ms. Odimpi.
(C) Ms. Raphael.
(D) Mr. Harada.

195. What type of position is Mr. Xavier probably interviewing for?
(A) Pastry chef.
(B) Restaurant manager.
(C) Business writer.
(D) Bartender's assistant.

GO ON TO THE NEXT PAGE.

City of Tempe

Requests to Film on City Property

Permits for filming on city property are issued by the Tempe Department of Public Works. Application documents should be completed online at least two weeks in advance of the proposed filming date(s) to allow adequate time for review. Read the following carefully before completing the application.

- Fill in every portion of the form. If not applicable, write "N/A".

- Describe each location and exactly what you plan to film there. Be specific.

- All production companies must pay a nonrefundable application fee of $500.

- Charitable organizations or individuals working on private projects are charged an application fee of $250.

- If amplified sound is used, proof of a noise permit will be required.

- If filming impedes pedestrians' ability to use a sidewalk, a traffic-control officer must be hired at the applicant's expense.

Application for Filming Permit

CITY OF TEMPE ARIZONA

Applicant information

The cabin crew were serving beverages to the passengers.

Name

Rino Pescatore

犀牛的簡稱. rhinoceros
红a33

Phone

554-1393

Address

1780 E University Ave,
Tempe, AZ 88003

Company

Name n/a

拍攝目的和活動大綱 , n,總結,摘要 adj,概括的,即時的,草率的

Purpose of Filming and Summary of Activities:

是在念大學的   影片製作者   工作團隊
期末作品   2個場景

I am an undergraduate filmmaker at Arizona State University, and
this is part of my final project. My crew will be filming two scenes at
Apodaca Park: one scene in the garden behind the Mesilla Valley Polo
                              濱   彼此追逐   在人行道上
Club, and one scene that will involve actors chasing each other on the
沿著
sidewalk along Mesilla Valley Drive at the Apodaca Boathouse. We
        手持的相機   /三腳架 三車
will have handheld cameras, a tripod, three vehicles, and minimal
                                红a
lighting equipment, but no sound equipment. Our only props will be
                              沒有   /properties 道具
an umbrella, a hockey stick, and a shovel.   最小的(最小限度的)
照明設備   音響設備
                        鏟子
                        挖土機

Filming Schedule:

Date	Location	Start/End Times	Number of Cast/Crew
April 9	Polo Club garden	8:00 A.M.—Noon	3-7 people
April 10	Mesilla Valley Drive at Apodaca Boathouse	8:00 A.M.—Noon	3-10 people

GO ON TO THE NEXT PAGE.

43

(A) 寄給公園管理員
(B) 貼在每一個拍攝點
(C) 在他大學裡歸檔
(D) 繳交給他的保險公司

(A) 需要特殊噪音許可
(B) 一位市府檢查員會來看
(C) 需要交通控管協助
(D) 是一位大學的員工

CITY OF TEMPE · ARIZONA

City of Tempe
Special Use Permit #002-0214

Rino Pescatore _____ of _____ 1780 E University Ave, Tempe, AZ 88003
(Name of Permittee)   **(Address)**

特此 授權

is hereby authorized to use Apodaca Park during the period of <u>April 9 — April 10</u>
between the hours of <u>8:00 a.m.</u> and <u>10:30 a.m.</u> for the purpose of <u>a university film</u>
<u>project</u>.

Specific locations: <u>Polo Club Garden and Mesilla Valley Drive at Apodaca Boathouse</u>
Maximum number of people: <u>10</u>   **Maximum number of vehicles:** <u>3</u>
Permittee Signature: *Rino Pescatore* _____   **Print Name:** <u>Rino Pescatore</u>
Authorizing Official Signature: *Mona Jarvis*   **Print Name:** <u>Mona Jarvis</u>

這張許可證必須被擺放(陳列)當在拍攝現場的所有時刻

Please note: This permit must be **displayed** at all times while on location. Violation
of the conditions state above will <u>result in</u> the permit being revoked.

違反者會導致許可證撤回   導致   revoke v. 撤回   違背·違反

196. What do the instructions indicate
about the Tempe Department of
Public Works? 申請作業時間超過一週
  (A) It requires more than one week
    to process permit applications.
  (B) It issues more permits to
    individuals than to production
    companies. 發出更多許可證給個人而非
  (C) It recommends that applications 製作公司
    be submitted by postal mail. →建議用郵寄的
  (D) It recently set limits on the
    number of permits issued per
    month. 最近設定每個月發放的許可證數量

197. What request of Mr. Pescatore was 只有部分獲
only partly allowed?   允許
  (A) The size of the group that he
    hoped could participate. 人數
  (B) The number of locations that he
    wished to use. 想用的場地
  (C) The amount of time that he
    wanted to be on-site. 在現場的時間
  (D) The amount of equipment that
    be wanted to bring. 想帶的設備

198. What is Mr. Pescatore required to do
with his permit?
  (A) E-mail it to the park managers.
  (B) Post it at each filming location.
  (C) Keep it on file at his university.
  (D) Submit it to his insurer.

199. What is mentioned in the instructions
about the city's permit applications fees?
  (A) They differ according to the location
    being filmed. 依地點有所不同
  (B) They will be returned if the permit is
    not issued. 證沒有通過可以退費
  (C) They can be paid in monthly
    installments. 可以按月分期付款
  (D) They are reduced for certain
    applicants 特別的申請者會減少(發得少)

200. What is implied about Mr. Pescatore?
  (A) He has a special noise permit.
  (B) He will be visited by a city inspector.
  (C) He will need traffic-control
    assistance.
  (D) He is an employee of a university.

**Stop! This is the end of the test. If you finish before time is called, you may go
back to Parts 5, 6, and 7 and check your work.**

New TOEIC Speaking Test

Question 1: Read a Text Aloud

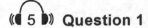 **Question 1**

Directions: In this part of the test, you will read aloud the text on the screen. You will have 45 seconds to prepare. Then you will have 45 seconds to read the text aloud.

The main point of this staff meeting is to <u>inform you</u> of some <u>developments</u> here at the department store in preparation for the start of the <u>holiday season</u>. We've moved our discounted items <u>toward the</u> front of the store to make room for the <u>seasonal products</u> that will soon begin arriving for display. <u>And speaking of the holiday season,</u> I know a lot of you will be looking to take time off to spend with your families. So, I have posted a vacation request sign-up sheet outside the management office. I can't guarantee every request will be filled, but I will do my best.

PREPARATION TIME
00 : 00 : 45

RESPONSE TIME
00 : 00 : 45

GO ON TO THE NEXT PAGE.

Question 2: Read a Text Aloud

Directions: In this part of the test, you will read aloud the text on the screen. You will have 45 seconds to prepare. Then you will have 45 seconds to read the text aloud.

The life of a career academic or postgraduate student typically does not lend itself easily to vacation and travel, making the opportunity to attend a scientific conference an attractive benefit.

A conference is a great opportunity to meet people in your field and put faces to names from publications. It is a great opportunity to network and meet the leaders in your field, collaborators, and potential supervisors or graduate students. Conferences also enable researchers to keep abreast of all advances in their field by presenting the latest research on a variety of subjects.

PREPARATION TIME
00 : 00 : 45

RESPONSE TIME
00 : 00 : 45

70

Question 3: Describe a Picture

Directions: In this part of the test, you will describe the picture on your screen in as much detail as you can. You will have 30 seconds to prepare your response. Then you will have 45 seconds to speak about the picture.

PREPARATION TIME

00 : 00 : 30

RESPONSE TIME

00 : 00 : 45

GO ON TO THE NEXT PAGE.→

Question 3: Describe a Picture

答題範例

3個年輕孩子為了拍照在擺姿勢
Three young children are posing for a picture.

They appear to be healthy. 他們看起來好像健康

They appear to be happy. 他們看起來好像開心

其中有二個小孩有戴頭巾
Two of the children are wearing headscarves.

One of the children is covering his or her face. 其中一個把臉遮起來

He or she might be camera-shy. 也有可能是對鏡頭害羞

左邊的孩子和中間的孩子看起來好像
The child on the left looks a lot like the child in the middle.

Maybe they are siblings. 他們可能是兄弟姊妹

They almost look like twins. 他們看起來幾乎是雙胞胎

背景是乾燥貧瘠的景觀
The background is a dry and barren landscape.

It's probably in the desert. 可能在沙漠裡

There is nothing to indicate where they might be.
沒有東西能指出他們可能在哪裡

The children have brown skin. 孩子們有深色肌膚

They also have dark eyes. 也有深色眼睛

All three are wearing jewelry such as bracelets and necklaces.
他們三個都有戴珠寶像是手環和項鍊

At least one child has multiple ear-piercings. 至少有1個孩子有好幾個耳洞

I'd say this is in the Middle East or Central Asia. 我會說是在中東或中亞

Another possibility is South America. 另外一個可能是在南美

72

Questions 4-6: Respond to Questions

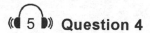 **Question 4**

Directions: In this part of the test, you will answer three questions. For each question, begin responding immediately after you hear a beep. No preparation time is provided. You will have 15 seconds to respond to Questions 4 and 5 and 30 seconds to respond to Question 6.

Imagine that a British marketing firm is doing research in your country. You have agreed to answer some questions in a telephone interview about your diet.

Question 4

On a scale of 1 to 10, how healthy is your diet?

RESPONSE TIME
00 : 00 : 15

Question 5

How much attention do you pay to nutritional information on packaged foods?

RESPONSE TIME
00 : 00 : 15

Question 6

Describe your favorite meal or type of food.

RESPONSE TIME
00 : 00 : 30

GO ON TO THE NEXT PAGE.

Questions 4-6: Respond to Questions

答題範例

🎧 6 Question 4

diet /ɪzɪ/ n. 飲食

On a scale of 1 to 10, how healthy is your diet?

room n. 房間, 空間

1到10分, 你的飲食有多健康?

improvement n. 改進, 改善

Answer

我會說, 大概只是5分

> I'd say I'm about a 5.
>
> I try to eat as healthy as possible. 我會嘗試盡量吃得健康
>
> But I'm sure there's room for improvement.

但我確定仍然有改進的空間。

improvement ⟷ deterioration
/dɪ,tɪrɪə'reʃən/
n. 惡化, 退化

🎧 6 Question 5

n. 注意力, 關注   付出   adj. 營養的   包裝食品

How much <u>attention</u> do you <u>pay</u> to <u>nutritional</u> information on <u>packaged foods</u>?

Answer

> Not that much, honestly. 不太多, 老實說
>
> Occasionally, I'll read the label. 有時候, 我會看標籤
>
> I sometimes check for sodium content.

我有時候會看
鈉   n. 內容, 專員
        content v. 使滿足
              adj. 滿足的

Questions 4-6: Respond to Questions

《《 6 》》 **Question 6**

描述你最喜歡的餐點或是食物種類

Describe your favorite meal or type of food.

Answer

我最喜愛的菜餚是中菜

/ KWĬZĬNI

My favorite type of cuisine is Chinese.

No other type of food comes close. 沒有其他種類的食物能
接近（我喜歡中菜的程度）

It is my comfort food.

吃中菜會讓我開心、舒服　＊comfort food 通常是高油,脂肪
不健康的食物

Chinese cuisine is very versatile. adj.多才多藝的
ヴ ヌ l ·易變的（很多種口味）

There are very light dishes like a simple noodle soup.

有很輕淡的菜像是簡單的麵湯

There are also very hearty dishes, for instance, hot pot.

也有非常豐盛的菜比如像火鍋

中菜　　強調　　新鮮度　味道

Chinese cuisine emphasizes freshness and flavor.

只用最好的材料

Only the best ingredients are used.

Every dish is prepared with great care. 每一道菜都用心製作

GO ON TO THE NEXT PAGE.

《 5 》 **Question 7**

Directions: In this part of the test, you will answer three questions based on the information provided. You will have 30 seconds to read the information before the questions begin. For each question, begin responding immediately after you hear a beep. No additional preparation time is provided. You will have 15 seconds to respond to Questions 7 and 8 and 30 seconds to respond to Question 9.

免費研討會   groom v.打扮·穿戴 n.新郎

FREE SEMINAR* →打扮寵物訓練
Pet Grooming Training
元 粗毛   厭煩-直花大錢幫寵物美容

Do you have a cat or a dog with a shaggy coat of fur? Are you tired of paying expensive grooming fees? Would you like to learn how to groom your pet yourself? Learn how to turn the anxiety of grooming into a bonding time for you and your pet.

焦慮 掛念 /æŋ'zɪɪətɪ/ We will teach you: 維繫感情的時刻

NAIL AND FUR MAINTENENCE ● DENTAL CARE ● MASSAGE THERAPY
指甲和毛維修(修剪) **Who are we?** 牙齒照顧   按摩治療

Danny and Tanya Smith are an animal loving couple who have volunteered their time for the protection of animals for more than 20 years. Their San Francisco-based pet spa Pampered Paws was voted #1 in the animal care category for Northern California's Best Small Businesses four years <u>in a row</u> (2008-2011).

*pamper v.紛寵愛(寵愛)   **How to attend?** 而子   一個接一個(連續)

Visit our website: <u>www.pawspetspa.com</u> for more information
or call Danny Smith at (415)454-2222

需要預約
*<u>Reservations required</u>. Though this event is offered free of charge, the organizers ask that you bring a pet food (or monetary) donation for the local animal shelter.

雖然這個活動不收費,還是希望你帶寵物食物或是金錢捐獻給當地寵物

Hi, I'm interested in the free pet grooming seminar. May I ask a few questions?

避難所。

PREPARATION TIME
00 : 00 : 30

Question 7	Question 8	Question 9
RESPONSE TIME	RESPONSE TIME	RESPONSE TIME
00 : 00 : 15	00 : 00 : 15	00 : 00 : 30

Questions 7-9: Respond to Questions Using Information Provided

答題範例

你和動物有什麼樣的經驗？（照顧過，養過）

What kind of experience do you have with animals?

Answer

be involved with

涉及某種情況或活動／熱中某事／和某人關係緊密

My wife and I have been involved with animals for over 20 years. 我和我太太和動物為伍超過20年了

擁有　經營　　寵愛寵物　　沙龍

We own and operate the Pampered Pets animal spa.

被票選為

Pampered Pets has been voted Northern California's #1 第名

Small Business four years in a row.

有任何小技巧可以處理這個

My dog's fur is always matted and tangled. Will there be any tips to deal with

問題嗎？

this problem?　纏結的　糾纏的

Answer

Yes. 我們會展現（教）你如何恰當的幫寵物洗頭．洗澡

We will be showing you how to shampoo and bathe your

pet properly.　　　　i.洗澡

We will also show you how to <u>prevent</u> your dog's fur <u>from</u>

matting.　　prevent from

教你如何防止你寵物毛髮打結

GO ON TO THE NEXT PAGE.

Questions 7-9: Respond to Questions Using Information Provided

《《 6 》) **Question 9**

Is there a fee for the seminar?

Answer

*enquire into 調查
about 查詢
for 去見
after 問候

這個研討會本身是免費的
The seminar itself is free.
我們休閒時間會做這件事
Tanya and I do this in our free time.
這和賺錢無關
It's not about making money.

然而, 我們要去註冊(登記)
However, we do require registration.

e   只是讓我們知道
你會來
That's just so we know you'll be there.

We don't want to waste anybody's time.
我們不想浪費任何人的時間

同時, 我們會要去參加者   常 捐獻物品
Meanwhile, we do ask that participants bring a donation
人
for the animal shelter. 給動物收容之家

This could be pet food or money.

There are some other ideas for donations on our Web

site.

Question 10: Propose a Solution

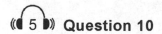 **Question 10**

Directions: In this part of the test, you will be presented with a problem and asked to propose a solution. You will have 30 seconds to prepare. Then you will have 60 seconds to speak. In your response, be sure to show that you recognize the problem, and propose a way of dealing with the problem.

In your response, be sure to

• show that you recognize the caller's problem, and

• propose a way of dealing with the problem.

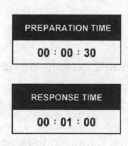

PREPARATION TIME
00 : 00 : 30

RESPONSE TIME
00 : 01 : 00

GO ON TO THE NEXT PAGE.

Question 10: Propose a Solution

答題範例

Voice Message

我打來找 Todd.　　　　　　　　　　是關於週五三點的事 (下午)

Hi, this is Steve calling for Todd. It's about three on Friday

聽著，　　　　我突然有事出現 (突然冒出)

afternoon. Listen, Todd. I had something come up at the

我無法如同原本規劃的和你還有 Sandra 見面

last-minute, so I won't be able to meet with you and Sandra on

我想要改在這周晚一點的時間

Monday as we had planned. I'd like to reschedule for later in

如果你們可以的話　　　　周二or四下午晚一點我可以

the week, if that works for you and Sandra. I'm available late

但周三五早上早點其實是最好

Tuesday and Thursday afternoons, but early morning

的時間

Wednesday or Friday would actually be best for me. We could

我們仍然可以在 Sandra 的辦公室見面，如同之前規劃的

still meet at Sandra's office, as we planned, or I'd be able to

或者約在其他你方便的所地

meet somewhere else if it's more convenient for you. Sorry

抱歉我的取消　　　麻煩你一聽到留言馬上回我電話

about the cancellation. Please call me as soon as you can

after hearing this. My cell is 886-2468, or you can call my office

at 351-9823 and leave a message. Thanks, Todd. I'll talk to you

soon.

Question 10: Propose a Solution

答題範例

Hello Steve.

I got your message and I'm returning your call.

Rescheduling is not a problem. 重新安排會面時間不是個問題

again

As it turns out, I would have had to cancel the meeting anyway.
如同結果一樣（取消會議）　我也會取消會議不管怎樣

Something came up on my end, too. 我最後也有事情要忙)

So don't apologize. 所以不要道歉

映過去事實/事物
的判斷或者揣測)
(我當時也會取消)

Let me check with Sandra about next week.

I know her schedule is pretty full. 我知道她行程很滿

But I'm sure we can work something out. 我們可以想出辦事法

理想地狀況，我們週四下午會見面
Ideally, we could meet Thursday afternoon.

Later in the week works best for me. 這週晚一點對我來說最好

It gives me a little more breathing room. 給我一些喘息的時間
/ˈbriðɪŋ/

如同 一開始計劃的
We'll meet in Sandra's office as originally planned.

I think that's best for everyone. 對每個人來說都好

And she has video conferencing in case we want to contact the investors.
以防　　　　連絡投資者

So let's play it by ear. 見機行事

Give me a call on Monday, by which time I'll have talked to Sandra.

Enjoy your weekend.

GO ON TO THE NEXT PAGE.

Question 11: Express an Opinion

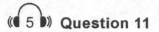 **Question 11**

Directions: In this part of the test, you will give your opinion about a specific

topic. Be sure to say as much as you can in the time allowed.

You will have 15 seconds to prepare. Then you will have 60

seconds to speak.

（整年天氣都很溫暖的地方）

有些人　　比較喜歡住在　溫暖　氣候　整年　　　然而
Some people prefer to live in warm climates all year round. However,

研究顯示　犯罪率　　比較高　在較溫暖的氣候度n
studies show that crime rates are much higher in warmer climates. Do you

覺得　人們　在溫暖氣候裡　導致較快乐的生活嗎
think that people in warm climates lead happier lives or not? State your

opinion and provide reasons for support.

陳述你的意見和提供理由支持你的論點

```
┌─────────────────────┐
│  PREPARATION TIME   │
├─────────────────────┤
│    00 : 00 : 15     │
└─────────────────────┘

┌─────────────────────┐
│   RESPONSE TIME     │
├─────────────────────┤
│    00 : 01 : 00     │
└─────────────────────┘
```

答題範例

我覺得一個可靠的(確定的,穩固的)平衡是快樂生活的關鍵
I think a certain balance is the key to a happy life.

這個觀念適用於每件事情,包括天氣
This applies to everything, including the weather.

Sometimes you can have too much of a good thing. 好事過頭反而成了壞事
= excess may do you harm

太陽太久,人們會躲到陰影裡
When it is sunny for too long, people head to the shade.

但是,如果開始下幾天雨,人們開始抱怨
But, if it rains for a few days, people complain.

It's a lose-lose situation. 是個雙輸的局面

我覺得 超級 冷的天氣 會 讓 人 變糟(慘,不好)
I think extremely cold weather can make people miserable, though.

When it is too cold, you shiver. 太冷的時候,你發抖

You can't go outside and all your energy is spent trying to get warm.
你不能去外面,然後你所有的力氣都拿去嘗試變溫暖(身體)

However, you have to take the good with the bad. 好壞兼收(不能只要好處)

較高的犯罪率是拿來交換 舒服的天氣
Higher crimes rates are a trade-off for comfortable/weather.

我想住在好氣候裡的人會明白這點
I would think that people in warmer climates understand this.

個人而言,我覺得住在較暖氣候的人比較快樂
Personally, I think people in warmer climates may be happier.

他們可以少煩腦一件事 一樣保持溫暖
They have one less thing to worry about; staying comfortable.

這是我的意見,但是當天氣好,太陽閃耀,的確比較會微笑
It's just my opinion but it's easier to smile when the sun's shining.

住在冷氣候的人們傾向比較保守
People in cold climates tend to be conservative.

They also tend to have narrow minds. 他們也傾向比較心胸狹窄

They don't seem happy to me. 對我而言,他們看起來不快樂

GO ON TO THE NEXT PAGE.

New TOEIC Writing Test

Questions 1-5: Write a Sentence Based on a Picture

Question 1

Directions: Write ONE sentence based on the picture using the TWO words or phrases under it. You may change the forms of the words and you may use them in any order.

dog / surfboard

1. The dogs are on the surfboard.
2. Two dogs are on the surfboard.
3. A man is teaching two dogs how to stand on a surfboard.

＊surf n. 海浪.浪花　　surf the internet
　　　v. 衝浪.瀏覽　　　上網

GO ON TO THE NEXT PAGE.

Questions 1-5: Write a Sentence Based on a Picture

Question 2

Directions: Write ONE sentence based on the picture using the TWO words or phrases under it. You may change the forms of the words and you may use them in any order.

board / children

1. Some children are boarding the bus.
2. The children are | a school bus.
   lined up and waiting to board the bus.

{ line up   { wait in line
{ queue up   { stand in line   排隊

The line / queue starts here. 隊伍從這裡開始
Don't cut / jump the line.   不要插隊
Could we form 2 files to the store, please. 移動中的隊伍

Questions 1-5: Write a Sentence Based on a Picture

Question 3

Directions: Write ONE sentence based on the picture using the TWO words or phrases under it. You may change the forms of the words and you may use them in any order.

music / students

1. The students are playing music.
2. The students are learning a piece of music.
一段音樂
3. Some students are performing music.

＊ music n. 音樂, 樂曲, 音樂作品
美妙的聲音. The music of the bird sounds very
sweet.

GO ON TO THE NEXT PAGE.

Questions 1-5: Write a Sentence Based on a Picture

Question 4

Directions: Write ONE sentence based on the picture using the TWO words or phrases under it. You may change the forms of the words and you may use them in any order.

couple / married

1. The couple have just been married.
2. The newly married couple are leaving the church.
3. The married couple are surrounded by friends and well-wishers.

* married adj. 已婚的 : Is she married?

　　　　　　婚姻的 : Her married life is exceptionally happy.

　　v. 結婚 　He is going to marry
　　　嫁娶　　　　　　　 Joanne.

Questions 1-5: Write a Sentence Based on a Picture

Question 5

Directions: Write ONE sentence based on the picture using the TWO words or phrases under it. You may change the forms of the words and you may use them in any order.

airport / gates

1. People are heading for their gates at the airport.
2. There are 36 B gates at the airport.
3. There is a smoking lounge located near Gate B 15 at the airport.

＊gate n. 大門, 登機門 ⟶ 勤奮是通往成功之路

路徑＝Diligence is the gate to success.

觀眾數＝Gates are down on last season.

上個賽季觀眾人數少了

GO ON TO THE NEXT PAGE.

Questions 6-7: Respond to a written request

Question 6

Directions: Read the e-mail below.

From: Kane Lightfoot <k_lightfoot@coheed.com>

To: Rani Ahmad <r_ahmad@inmail.com>

Re: Part-time opportunity

Sent: January 31

However, Although, Notwithstanding

Dear Ms. Ahmad,

真誠的 感謝   面試   資深 網頁 行政管理者
We sincerely appreciate you interviewing for the senior Web
    的職位   然而   很遺憾的通知
administrator position at Coheed & Associates. However, I regret to
你   人事 部門   決定 選擇 另外一個
inform you that the personnel department decided to go with another
候選人   不過 我們對於你的知識和經驗印象深刻
candidate. Nevertheless, we were impressed by the knowledge and
     你在面試時所展現出來的   決定
experience that you displayed during your interview and have decided
給你另外一個最近空出來的職位
to offer you another recently-vacated position.

和你申請的工作相比,   這個職位是兼差的
In contrast to the position you applied for, this position is part-time.

You would be working on Tuesday, Wednesday, and Friday from 1:00
to 5:00 PM and on Monday and Thursday from 2:00 to 6:00 PM.

If you are interested in this position, please call me at 555-0923 or
email me at k_lightfoot@coheed.com.   * candidate n 候選人

Sincerely,   * candidacy   n 候選資格
Kane Lightfoot   to announce one's candidacy 宣佈自己為候選人

回信   接受這個職位
Directions: Write back to Mr. Lightfoot and accept the position, but
要求   做的改變 針對 預訂好的工作時間
    request ONE minor change to the scheduled work hours.
    理由
    Give ONE reason for the request.

Questions 6-7: Respond to a written request

[handwritten:] ★ agreeable
adj 討人的, an agreeable odor 答題範例
令人愉快的   味道

Question 6

[handwritten:] ⊙ They were all agreeable to our proposal.
同意

Dear Mr. Lightfoot,

[handwritten:] = unlucky = ill-fated
可惜的.不幸的 ↔ fortunate

Thank you for your letter of January 31. It's unfortunate that the position I
[handwritten: 已經被填補]
applied for has been filled, but I would be very pleased to accept the new
[handwritten: 我在想你是否願意]
position that you are offering. However, I was wondering if you would be
[handwritten: 同意   小小的改變 關於   我上班的時間]
agreeable to a minor change regarding the hours I would be working.

[handwritten: 提到   我的志工經驗]
During my interview, I referenced my experience volunteering with World
Vision. I was recently offered a position working part time for them, but
[handwritten: 衝突:抵觸]
there is a schedule conflict. I work for them Tuesday, Wednesday, and
Thursday from 9:00 AM to 1:00 PM. Would it be possible for me to work
for you from 1:30 to 5:30 PM on Tuesday and Wednesday? If so, please
let me know at your earliest convenience. *[handwritten: 你一有空就讓我知道]*

[handwritten: 順便提一句   責任(工作內容)]
Incidentally, the duties that I currently perform for World Vision are exactly
the same as the responsibilities of the position with Coheed & Associates.
So, I believe that I would adjust very quickly to working for Coheed.
[handwritten: 我很快就會適應這裡的工作]

I look forward to becoming a valuable member of Coheed & Associates.

[handwritten: 和不熟的人的結尾]   *[handwritten: 和熟的人 All the best!]*
Sincerely,   *[handwritten: Talk to you later!]*
[handwritten: / Best regards,]
Rani Ahmad

Question 7

Directions: Read the e-mail below.

From: Shirley Jackson <cc_jackson@shaker.com>
To: Sunburst Airlines Claims <claims@sunburstairline.com>
Date: June 15
Subject: Claim # SA345
Attachments: jackson.jpg; jackson2.jpg; jackson3.jpg

To whom it may concern: 敬啟者

*submit ㄑ繳交
under send
便服従. 便屈服

On May 19, I traveled from Newark, New Jersey, to Orlando, Florida, on Sunburst Airlines Flight 810. My bag arrived on a different flight and was delivered to my home only a few hours ago. The contents were fine, but the exterior of the bag was badly damaged. The case was dented. The suitcase is no longer usable as it cannot be closed properly. On May 21, I submitted claim form number SA345. I understood that I would take up to two weeks for the claim to be processed, but it is now June 15 and I have not had any response.

Please let me know how this problem will be resolved. As I did with the original claim, I am attaching a photo of the damaged property and photocopies of my boarding pass and baggage claim tickets.

Shirley Jackson

Directions: Reply to Ms. Jackson as Kirby Little, Claims Manager of Sunburst Airlines. Tell her that you've resolved her issue and offer ONE thing in return for the inconvenience. Also include TWO ways of contacting you.

答題範例

Question 7

Ms. Jackson,

Thank you for submitting your claim to Sunburst Airlines. We deeply 我們深的感到遺憾
在處理您要求時造成的延誤(延誤)   在看完文件之後
regret the delay in processing your request. After reviewing the
我已經同意你的申請而且發出全額賠償
documentation, I have approved your claim and have issued full
賠   對於去失及和行李受損   全額支票
償 restitution for both losing and damaging your baggage. A check for the
已經郵寄到你原始飛機預訂資料中列下的地址
total amount has been mailed to the address listed on your original
由於   造成 不便   自由權
flight reservation. In light of the inconvenience, I have taken the liberty
of including an Sunburst Airlines Voucher of $200 value toward a flight
ticket redeemable within the next six months.

adj·可贖回的, 可贖還的   redeem v. 買回, 贖回, 換回

Thank you for being a Sunburst Airlines passenger. If you have any
questions or concerns, please contact me directly either by email or the
number below.

(給你東西)

我已經自行使用權利包含
200的禮券關於6個月內可以兌換的
機票

Kirby Little

Claims Manager

(800)774-3300 ext. 98

GO ON TO THE NEXT PAGE.

Questions 8: Write an opinion essay

Question 8

Directions: Read the question below. You have 30 minutes to plan, write, and revise your essay. Typically, an effective response will contain a minimum of 300 words.

想個工作你曾經有的或是想要的

就你的意見而言，

Think about a job you have had or would like to have. In your

哪些是重要的特質，是你，和你一起工作的人在這工作中

opinion, what are the most important characteristics that you and the

獲得成功需具備的？

people you work with should possess to be successful in that job? Use

reasons and specific examples to illustrate why these characteristics are

important. 給出理由和具體的例子去說明為何這些特質是重要的

* character
æ ɪ æ
m 品質、性格

characteristic
æ ə ɔ ɪ ɪ
n. 特徵，特色

adj. 特有的，獨特的

如何舉例：

Some examples include
One clear example of this is
For example

如何表達認同

(I strongly / firmly believe
I'm completely in favor of

(In my opinion,
If I had to choose, I would say
I would prefer to

不認同

(I'm totally opposed to
I really don't agree with

Questions 8: Write an opinion essay

答題範例

*set apart 使與眾不同
使農夫和農場經營者與眾不同

Question 8

n.食譜,方法 農業領域要成功沒有方法(沒有公式),但專家認同特定的特質

There is no recipe for success in farming, but experts agree certain qualities set successful farmers and ranchers apart, including passion, a positive attitude, the ability to handle adversity and "gut instinct." Successful producers also embrace change and maintain a can-do attitude. When problems arise, they come up with solutions instead of excuses. They also have a good understanding of local and global markets and the issues facing their industry. 他們企業(行業)面對到的問題

The first quality of a successful farmer is learning how to manage money. Most farmers start small, keeping costs down and doing a lot of the construction work themselves. People in business need to start small with any new venture so that the mistakes are small enough that they can adjust and survive. 可以調整和生存

Next, innovation has always been a big part of farming. The ups and downs of growing commodity crops have become more frequent and severe. Taking a different path and producing for markets with specific needs offers a better chance at evening out the peaks and valleys. The ability to adapt to market changes is key; resourcefulness will help a business survive when times are tough.

Third, time management is important in any business, but it's crucial in farming, where outside factors such as weather have a huge impact. Whether it's bad weather or equipment breakdowns, a producer has to be ready to switch from plan A to plan B, or C or D.

Fourth, as a business gets larger, strong communication and people skills are also necessary so every part of the operation is being managed properly. Good operators have other good people in their corner. Playing to your strengths improves efficiencies and saves headaches. Hire someone who's good at the things you're not good at or don't care to do.

Finally, the most important quality of a farmer is attention to detail. A dairy farmer, for example, must always be checking cows, milk charts, rations, feed costs and markets— keeping abreast of everything and looking for areas that can be improved. You have to pay attention to the growing side of things for peak production, but marketing a product also demands a great deal of time and attention to detail. Producing, processing, and marketing produce requires both physical and mental attention. It's attention to small details that makes you or breaks you. If you don't pay attention to the small details, they can turn into large problems. Given the high price of agricultural products, mistakes are very expensive.
有鑑於農業的高成本,錯誤是非常昂貴的